MW01483886

# GHOSTLY DISTRESS

*A Harper Harlow Mystery Book Nine*

# LILY HARPER HART

HarperHart Publications

Copyright © 2018 by Lily Harper Hart

All rights reserved.

No part of this book may be reproduced in any form or by any electronic or mechanical means, including information storage and retrieval systems, without written permission from the author, except for the use of brief quotations in a book review.

❀ Created with Vellum

## ONE

"I can't believe this is how it's going to end."

Zander Pritchett, his handsome face somber and streaked with dirt, leaned his back against a tombstone and snagged his best friend's gaze. He was completely spent ... and resigned.

For her part, the best friend in question, Harper Harlow, remained wary. "Who said anything about anything ending?" she challenged, her honey blond hair tucked behind her ear as she regarded the man who had stood by her since kindergarten with something akin to suspicion. "Why do you have to make everything so dramatic, Zander? There's no reason to turn this into a big thing."

"Really?" Zander wasn't one to go down without a fight. "You don't think there's a reason to be dramatic. Look where we are." He extended his hands and gestured toward the familiar surroundings. Whisper Cove Cemetery sometimes felt like a second home, which Zander remained bitter about. "You don't think there's a legitimate reason for me to be dramatic?"

Harper wrinkled her forehead as she glanced around. "Not really." She was understandably confused. They were ghost hunters, by trade and cosmic design. The cemetery was a frequent stop on their travels for Ghost Hunters, Inc. (or GHI to the inner circle), the business they owned together. Now, since it was so very close to Halloween, they were spending even more time than usual at the facility because they'd started up their lucrative side business: ghost tours. "This is a normal day in our world."

Zander ran his tongue over his lips as he shifted, making sure to remain behind the ornate tombstone that he chose for cover while giving Harper his full attention. "This is so not a normal day."

Harper was genuinely perplexed by the serious expression on her best friend's face. "How do you figure that?"

"Well, for starters, we're sitting in a cemetery hoping to see ghosts." Zander gestured toward a plastic wreath as it went whizzing by his head, managing to appear calm despite the fact that he felt the exact opposite.

"How is that any different from what we usually do?" Harper argued. "We own a ghost-hunting business. You remember GHI, right? Your name is on the articles of incorporation as co-owner."

Zander made a face. "We didn't file articles of incorporation. It wasn't necessary for such a small business." He was GHI's official accountant so he took business comments – even offhand ones – very seriously.

Harper rolled her eyes. "You know what I mean."

"Not really." Zander wasn't in the mood to play nice. In fact, the exact opposite. He wanted to torture his best friend until she gave in and saw things his way. That was the mark of a good relationship ... er, well, at least in his book. "I have no idea what you mean. In fact, I'm often baffled by anything you have to say. I don't think you're the best communicator."

Harper narrowed her eyes until they were nothing more than glittery slits. "Well, if you feel we need to communicate more clearly ... "

Zander recognized the glint for what it was. "Oh, don't go turning evil. I'm not to blame for this little snafu." He ducked his head again when a plastic flower bounced off the tombstone and caused him to inadvertently cringe. "That was just tacky."

Harper pursed her lips as she shifted and craned her neck to look over the much smaller tombstone she hid behind. "Yeah. Randy is in quite the mood tonight. I guess we didn't need to rile him for the tour after all."

"I don't see why we ever rile him," Zander groused. "I would think riling up a ghost is a bad idea."

"Randy is basically harmless," Harper reminded him. "We're conducting a ghost tour in ten minutes." She double-checked her watch to be sure. "That means people will start arriving in five minutes. We need ghosts on our tour. You know that. The only one who is always willing to show up and perform on cue is Randy. That's not my fault. I don't create the ghosts, or tell them where to be at a certain time. We have to work with what we've got."

Zander offered his best friend an exaggerated face that was so ridiculous Harper had to bite back a laugh despite her annoyance. "Do you really think I'm upset about Randy?"

"You once told me you were affronted by his name and we should cut him from the yearly tours."

Zander scowled. "I still maintain that his name is stupid," he muttered. "I mean ... Randy is a ridiculous name for so many reasons. When you add his last name, though – Randy Johnson – it's beyond absurd. That's not really why I'm angry, though, and you know it."

Harper knit her eyebrows. "If you're not upset about Randy and his penchant for throwing ugly cemetery decorations, why are you upset?" She was genuinely curious.

"You know why."

"If I knew, I wouldn't have asked."

Zander was nothing if not stubborn and the look he graced Harper with as he folded his arms across his chest and ignored the small placard that bounced off the top of his head was downright scorching. "I'm angry because you're abandoning me."

Now it was Harper's turn to make a face. "Abandoning you?"

"You heard me." Zander jutted out his square chin. "You're moving out and abandoning me. It's as if we're not even friends and I don't count. I mean ... how could you?" He sounded legitimately wounded. "You were my soulmate ... just not in a gross sexual way."

Harper exhaled heavily as she regarded the one person who had always been there for her no matter the circumstances. Realizing you can see and talk to ghosts is a scary thing and it didn't exactly make Harper popular throughout high school. Zander stood by her through all of that, not only serving as her anchor but also opting to believe she could do what she said she could without any real proof. He was loyal that way.

That's what Harper reminded herself now as she fought the urge to throw herself on him in an effort to dislodge him from his safe place and let Randy the rabble-rouser pelt him with plastic flowers and decorations.

"I'll ignore the part about you being grossed out about having sex with me," Harper muttered.

"Oh, puh-leez." Zander rolled his eyes so hard Harper worried he would topple to his left. "You don't find me attractive in that manner any more than I find you attractive. Although ... at least I have the right parts to turn you on. You're severely lacking for me. Maybe you really are turned on by me and simply sad you can't have me. That would explain a few things." He thoughtfully tapped his bottom lip. "Wait ... what were we talking about again?"

"How you're being a pain about Jared and me moving in together and I've had it," Harper snapped, refusing to let Zander sidetrack the conversation. "You said you were fine with it when it first came up – happy even – and now all I hear from you is whining and complaints. I don't get it."

"If you don't understand I certainly can't explain it to you," Zander sniffed, averting his eyes.

Harper was officially at the end of her rope. "You're just being difficult to be difficult. I don't understand. Jared said he talked to you about this before he even mentioned it to me. You were fine with it at the time. What changed?"

Zander shrugged, noncommittal. "Maybe I've simply had time to think things through more clearly and I don't think moving in with your boyfriend is the way to go. I think you should stay with me."

"We're moving across the road, Zander!" Harper snapped, her temper finally winning the battle and making an appearance. "We're going to be so close we'll be able to talk to one another from our front porches. It's the best possible solution to our living situation. I don't understand why you can't see that."

"Because it results in you and I no longer sharing a roof."

"But we'll be so close." Harper rarely wanted to physically harm Zander, but she was battling the urge now. Instead of acting on that impulse, though, she adopted a pragmatic approach. "You agreed that things were going to turn ugly if we didn't separate one four-person household into two two-person households. Jared came up with the perfect solution where we can see each other whenever we want and it also happens to allow him and Shawn privacy. I don't understand what the big deal is."

"The big deal is that you won't allow me to help you decorate and you're tragically color blind when it comes to painting and picking out furniture," Zander huffed. "You know it's pure torture for me when you have furniture and design catalogs and I'm not allowed to make decisions."

Harper's spine stiffened as she swiped at her cheek and ignored the plastic rose that smacked against it. "That's what is bothering you? You're upset because I want to decorate my own house?"

Zander merely shrugged. "I'm better when it comes to decorating than you. We both know it."

"Oh, whatever." Harper frowned as she slowly stood and extended a warning finger in Randy's direction. She was the only one who could see his ethereal figure and she was tired of his antics. "Save some of it for the tour, Randy. You're going to run out of supplies at this rate."

Randy, a former logger who died in the seventies and refused to cross over no matter how many times Harper offered to help out his restless soul, merely sneered. "It's a big cemetery. I won't run out of things to throw at you."

Harper flicked a glance to the parking lot where tonight's tour patrons were already starting to gather. "Good to know." She took a step in that direction, completely ignoring Zander as he scrambled to follow. "See you in a little bit, Randy. Thanks for always being reliable."

"I am not reliable!" Randy shot back, indignant. "I am terrifying. I rule this cemetery."

"Yeah, yeah." Harper waved off the statement and refused to make eye contact with Zander as he pulled even with her. "You and I are going to have a big talk later."

Most men would've been terrified by Harper's tone, but Zander was hardly the type to wilt under pressure. "I'm looking forward to it. What do you think about doing your kitchen in pink?"

"I think I'm going to make you cry before the night is out."

"Oh, so you're going with eggplant, aren't you?" Zander was horrified. "Now you're just being mean."

"Whatever."

**AS FAR AS TOURS** go, Harper knew tonight's offering wasn't her best show. She was still agitated with Zander and it took her a good ten minutes to relax into her shtick. Still, by the time the tour was concluding, Harper believed her guests were having a good time and she'd relaxed enough to stop plotting Zander's death whenever she had a free moment.

"How come we haven't seen any ghosts?"

Gary Conner, a middle-aged business owner who did something in an office that Harper couldn't quite seem to remember even though he told her the details no less than three times, appeared to be the lone individual intent on ruining the tour for everyone.

"I've already told you, Mr. Conner," Harper drawled, forcing herself to remain calm as she picked her way toward the parking lot. "Only certain people can see ghosts."

"You need the gift," Zander called out, opting to take Harper's side even though things were far from settled between them. "Harper has the gift. That's why she can see ghosts. You clearly don't have the gift."

Gary fixed Zander with a dubious look. "And do you have the gift?"

"I have many gifts." Zander understood taking out his frustrations on a paying customer was the wrong way to go, but he was very close to doing just that. "I can't see ghosts, but Harper can. Besides, you got hit in the head four times with plastic flowers. If that wasn't a ghost, what was it?"

Gary shrugged. "I'm sure it was some sort of fake magic you guys set up."

"Yes, because wasting our time throwing plastic flowers at people seems like a great way to spend a chilly October evening," Zander drawled, making a face when Harper pinned him with a warning look. "What? You're thinking the same thing."

Harper ignored Zander's outburst. She was used to his fits of whimsy. "I'm sorry you didn't have a good time, Mr. Conner. Maybe next year, huh?" He always attended at least one tour, which Harper didn't understand because the man was adamant ghosts weren't real. It was almost as if he wanted to participate simply to argue ... an inclination Harper couldn't wrap her head around.

Gary let loose a condescending look. "I'm sure there won't be a next year." He always said that ... and then he always came back.

As if on cue, a plastic flower pot smacked Gary on the forehead before harmlessly glancing to the side and hitting the ground.

"I still maintain you're somehow faking this," Gary muttered as he swiped at the dirt on his face. "There's no other explanation."

"There is an explanation," Colin Thompson argued, appearing at Harper's elbow and fixing Gary with an annoyed look. "The ghosts don't like you and that's why they're throwing things at you. I mean ... buy a clue."

Harper bit the inside of her cheek to keep from laughing at Colin's outraged expression. She'd known him since he was a teenager – he was twenty-three now but didn't look old enough to drink – and he'd been attending tours almost since she started offering them. Even though Harper was only four years older than the young man, sometimes it felt like they had a lifetime between them. Still, it was obvious Colin had a crush on Harper and she did nothing to dissuade it. In fact, she was mildly flattered by the attention.

"Thank you, Colin." Harper patted his arm and grinned as she forced herself to keep from pumping her fist as Gary continued to scowl and wipe at the side of his face. "It's always nice when you come to my aid. It's not necessary, though. If Mr. Conner doesn't believe in ghosts, he doesn't believe in ghosts. It's pretty simple."

"Well, he doesn't have to be rude about it." Colin glowered at Gary. "Just suck it up and be nice, man. You don't have to be a tool."

"I completely agree," Zander said, slinging an arm over Colin's shoulders. "You're always a bright spot in an otherwise colorless land-scape, Colin. Have I told you how happy I am you're still coming to the tours?"

Colin's smile was sheepish. "Oh, well, you know how I feel about ghosts." His gaze lingered on Harper, causing Zander to smirk.

"Yes, I know exactly how you feel about ghosts."

Gary made a growling sound in the back of his throat as he pulled away from the rest of the group. "This has been a complete waste of time. I can't believe I let myself be talked into this ... again. In fact ... ." He was just warming up for what Harper was certain would be a right-eous diatribe when he pitched forward and disappeared behind a large bush.

Harper pressed her lips together and swallowed the mad urge to laugh as she exchanged a quick look with Zander. He wasn't as strong as his co-worker and had to duck his head as snickers filled the air. Harper, on the other hand, immediately hurried to Gary's aid.

"Mr. Conner, are you okay?" She peered over the bush, expecting to find a furious guest who would most likely demand a refund. Instead, she found a white-faced man with shaking hands who looked as if he was about to pass out. "Mr. Conner, what is it?"

Gary didn't immediately answer, instead slowly extending a trem-bling finger and pointing. Harper followed the direction he pointed, her heart rolling when she realized Gary didn't trip because of karma. No, rather, he tripped because someone left a little something on the other side of the bush for him to trip over.

It just so happened to be a body.

"Oh, my." Harper managed to hold back a gasp as she stared into the sightless eyes of a young woman who looked to have died in a horrible manner. Harper could practically hear the scream frozen on the woman's pale lips. "I think we need to call the police."

Gary finally found his voice. "Oh, do you think? Where was your ghost to tell you about this?"

Harper didn't have an answer. It was a fairly good question, though. "I don't know."

# TWO

J ared Monroe widened his eyes from the passenger seat of his partner's cruiser and let loose a low growl when he saw the crowd milling about in the parking lot of Whisper Cove's main cemetery.

"What the ... ?"

"That's exactly what I was about to say." Though older and he liked to believe considerably wiser, Mel Kelsey was at a loss as he navigated around a group of excitable people and parked in a slot close to the gate. "What exactly did Harper say when she called?"

"She said to get here as soon as possible," Jared replied, furrowing his brow as he scanned the crowd for signs of his girlfriend. Even though he logically knew she was fine – she'd called him ten minutes before, after all – he wouldn't be able to ease his worry until he actually saw her. "She also said one of the tour patrons tripped over a body."

Mel made an annoyed sound in the back of his throat. He was used to Harper Harlow's special brand of drama. He'd known her since she was a child, after all. As Zander's uncle, he was familiar with both of them. That didn't mean he was keen for whatever theatrics he was about to bear witness to. "Are we sure it's a real body?"

Jared arched an eyebrow. "I don't see why she would lie."

"I'm not saying she's lying. I'm merely suggesting that perhaps she and Zander got worked up during a cemetery tour and thought they saw something that wasn't really there. It would hardly be the first time it happened."

Jared forced himself to remain calm. He often had to remind himself that Mel didn't gaze through the same adoring lenses when looking at Harper. To Jared, Harper was an absolutely delightful ball of energy who was not only full of love but also worthy of everything he had to offer. To Mel, Harper was the girl who used to run around causing mischief with Zander and still managed to wreak havoc a couple times a year when the mood struck.

"I think Harper knows what a real body looks like," Jared pointed out. "She's seen more than her fair share of bodies."

"She has but ... I just don't want to spend the rest of the night filling out paperwork," Mel groused. "I hate this time of year. We spend half our time patrolling for tricksters and the other half convincing people they're not really being haunted."

Jared licked his lips as regarded his taciturn partner. "You're a regular ray of sunshine sometimes. You know that, don't you?"

Mel shrugged. "Am I wrong?"

Sadly, Jared couldn't find footing to argue. "No, but I really wish you wouldn't cast aspersions on Harper. She's a good woman and she wouldn't have called if she really didn't find something important."

Mel didn't bother to hide his eye roll. "Yeah, yeah, yeah. The fact that you're whipped for your blonde isn't reason enough for me to assume she and Zander aren't being dramatic. I want to see this body for myself before I believe it."

"Fine. When you do see it, though, you're going to owe my girl an apology."

"We'll see."

**MEL UTTERED A** low curse when he caught sight of the young woman on the ground. She was clearly dead, her blue eyes glazed and sightless as they stared at the moon. Her arms were open, as if offering something to the night sky, and her body was contorted in such a way he knew it was impossible that she purposely put herself in that position.

"She's dead," Zander announced helpfully as Jared pulled Harper in for a quick hug.

"Thank you, Zander," Mel drawled, annoyed. "I never would've guessed that without your astute observation."

Zander offered his uncle a "you'll pay for that later" look before planting his hands on his hips. "I'm trying to be helpful."

"Well, you're not doing a very good job of it," Mel muttered, carefully kneeling next to the girl and using a short branch from the nearby bush to dig in the underbrush. "We need to call this in to the medical examiner's office."

"How do you even know she's dead?" Gary called out from the spot Harper forced him to stand once he recovered from the ordeal of tripping over a dead body. "You haven't given her CPR."

Jared smoothed the back of Harper's hair before releasing her, his eyes briefly pinning Gary before focusing on his girlfriend. "Are you okay?"

Harper forced a smile and nodded. "It was a good night other than Zander being a pain and ... well ... this." She gestured toward the body. "I wouldn't have even seen her if Gary hadn't decided to walk off in a huff. He walked away from the trail and tripped over her."

"You're welcome," Gary barked.

Jared arched an eyebrow and pressed his lips together to keep from laughing. It wasn't a humorous situation and yet he couldn't stop himself from being amused ... at least briefly. "Start at the beginning."

"Okay, we were on the tour and we were almost done," Harper started.

"And then Gary turned into a tool and made a scene because he thought we were faking Randy's obnoxious responses," Zander added. "Frankly, I blame him for all this."

"Yeah, because I'm the one who killed her and then tripped over the body to create an alibi," Gary deadpanned. "You're such a ... twink."

Zander's mouth dropped open and Jared had to hold up a hand to keep the man from screeching and causing a scene.

"We don't have time for this, Zander," Jared warned, keeping his voice low. "We have a murder in a cemetery that's been very busy over the past few days. If you want to be loud with your buddy Gary, you need to do it someplace else."

Zander had the grace to be abashed. "Fine." He flicked his eyes to Gary. "I'll meet you at high noon on Main Street."

Harper widened her eyes and ducked her head to hide her smile as she regrouped. The movement forced her to focus on the dead girl on the ground, which was instantly sobering. "How do you know she was murdered?"

"Because her neck is broken," Jared replied gently. "If it wasn't, she wouldn't be in that position. Do you see those bruises on her skin there?"

Harper followed Jared's finger and swallowed hard as she nodded.

"Someone strangled her, Heart." Jared calmly ran his hand over his girlfriend's slender back. "This wasn't an accident. I'm sorry if you thought it was."

"I knew it probably wasn't an accident," Harper conceded. "I guess I was hopeful because ... well, just because."

"I get that." Jared brushed a quick kiss against Harper's forehead before stepping away and studying the bush to his right. "Some of the branches are broken here. We should probably call out the state police tech team to have a look while we're at it. They might be able to get a footprint or something."

"Oh, that wasn't like that at the start," Zander offered. "Gary did that when he realized he tripped over a body. He was screaming like a girl when he clawed his way to freedom."

Zander looked so proud of himself for the proffered tidbit Jared had to look away to keep a straight face as he dug for his phone.

"I'm going to call for the medical examiner," Jared said. "I believe you should start with an apology to Harper, Mel."

Mel's eyebrows hopped. "Excuse me?"

"You said you thought she was being dramatic. She obviously wasn't being dramatic."

Mel scowled as Harper narrowed her eyes and shot a dark look in his direction. "You just couldn't let it go, could you?"

"Not when you're maligning my girlfriend, no."

Mel growled. "I'm sorry, Harper. I didn't mean to malign you."

Harper waved off the apology. "That's okay. I'm used to it."

"What about me?" Gary challenged. "Does anyone want to apologize to me?"

Harper ignored him and focused on Zander. "We should probably calm down the tour participants. They might be freaking out."

Zander brightened. "Good idea."


**JARED FOUND HARPER** leaning against the hood of her car, Zander tucked in close at her side, an hour later. The medical examiner remained busy with the body and the bulk of the tour patrons had departed save for Gary and Colin, both of whom refused to leave.

"You don't have to stay, Heart," Jared said quietly as he moved to stand in front of her. "There's nothing you can do here."

Harper tilted her head to the side as she regarded him. "You look tired."

"It's still early."

"You still look tired."

"You definitely do," Zander agreed, shifting so he could study Jared for an extended amount of time. "You're starting to get crow's feet. You're too young for that. See, Harp, this is another reason you shouldn't move in with him ... other than the eggplant kitchen, I mean."

Jared pressed the tip of his tongue against the back of his teeth. "I don't have crow's feet."

"Ignore him." Harper straightened. "Do you know who she is?"

Jared reluctantly dragged his eyes from Zander and nodded. "Mel recognized her. He said her name was Maggie Harris. She's twenty-five and ... ."

Jared didn't get a chance to finish because recognition dawned on Harper's face and she finished for him. "She worked at the bank."

Jared widened his eyes. "You knew her?"

"It's a small town. Everyone knows everyone."

"I guess." Jared shifted his gaze to where the medical examiner toiled. "We have to make notification after this. It's probably going to be a bit before I get home. You can leave now, though. I'll have reports for both of you to sign in the morning but it's pretty straightforward."

"We can wait," Harper offered.

"You don't have to. I'm not sure how long I'll be."

"Still, I don't want to go home without you," Harper persisted. "We can wait."

"Speak for yourself," Zander shot back. "I'm not waiting. Shawn is already at the house and he ordered pizza."

As if on cue, Harper's stomach growled at the news. She was too loyal to choose pizza over Jared, though. "Oh, well, I'm still waiting for Jared."

Jared considered messing with her, but the idea of Harper sitting outside in the dark and waiting for him to come to her was something he had trouble swallowing. "I think you should go home, Heart." Jared was firm. "Waiting for me isn't going to do you any good, especially since I have no idea how long all of this will take."

Harper wasn't quite done arguing. "But ... ."

"No." Jared leaned forward and gave her a quick kiss. "I insist you go home and eat your weight in pizza with Zander and Shawn. I prefer knowing you're safe."

"I can make sure she gets home safely," Colin offered as he popped up next to Jared and caused him to jolt. "That's the entire reason I'm still sticking close."

"Um ... ." Jared kept his arm around Harper's waist as he glanced around, confused. "I ... you ... who are you again?"

"Colin Thompson." Colin rubbed a hand over his short brown hair and kept his shoulders squared. "I'm here to protect Harper. Who are you?"

Even though they were at the scene of a murder, Harper couldn't stop herself from smirking at Jared's obvious discomfort. "This is Jared. He's Whisper Cove's newest police officer."

"He's also Harper's boyfriend, Colin," Zander added. "I know that's the last thing you want to hear but ... there it is. They're even moving in together."

Colin looked crushed. "What?"

Jared glanced between Colin and Zander for a moment, his mind struggling to put things together. "Am I missing something?"

"No," Harper answered automatically.

"Yes." Zander and Colin bobbed their heads in unison.

"Oh, joy." Jared pressed the heel of his hand to his forehead and worked overtime to come to grips with the situation. "Can someone give me a very brief summary?"

Zander shot his hand into the air and hopped up and down. "Pick me!"

Jared growled. "I'm going to regret this. I just know it." He jerked his thumb in Zander's direction. "Tell me in as few words as possible. I'm not joking."

"Okay." Zander rubbed his hands together, relishing his spot as center of attention. "Basically, it breaks down as this: Colin has been a huge fan of GHI since we started. That was five years ago, though, and he was only eighteen at the time."

"A *mature* eighteen," Colin stressed.

Zander grinned as he nodded. "Definitely a mature eighteen. Anyway, he was along for our inaugural cemetery tour right after starting GHI. He comes back every year even though he's a big college student now."

"I graduated," Colin corrected. "I'm no longer a college student."

"Oh." Zander was appropriately impressed. "Does that mean you're back home living with your mother because you can't find a job or you love Harper so much you made a special trip? Wait ... I'm not sure which one I want more. Let me think for a second."

Jared scowled as he flicked Zander's ear. "I'm still behind and I'm starting to get agitated."

"You're not the only one," Colin shot back. "Are you really Harper's boyfriend?" He didn't wait for an answer before swiveling to face Harper. "Why do you have a boyfriend? I told you to wait for me."

Harper was contrite. "I've always found you cute, Colin, but you're too young for me."

"I'm only four years younger than you."

"It's closer to five years."

Colin turned pouty. "I don't really care about that," he muttered. "I just don't see why you need a boyfriend. It's not really like I expected you to date me or anything. I'm not a stalker. I just ... he's a police officer."

Colin looked so horrified it caused Zander to chuckle. "A police officer?" Colin remained incredulous. "I'm going to be a finance manager. No joke. I just have to find a job and then I'm on my way."

Jared tried not to be offended, but he couldn't help himself. "You're going to be a finance manager? What are you doing until then?"

"Finance manager on weekends," Colin answered, primly smoothing his shirt.

Jared felt mildly irritated by the young man's bravado – and his attitude regarding cops didn't help – but even he found the goofy kid entertaining. "Well, that's great. What do you do on weekdays?"

"I'm a chef."

"A chef, huh? Where?"

"Does that matter?" For the first time since he arrived for the tour, Colin let his temper out to play. "I mean ... I'm a food connoisseur. You shoot people for a living."

"I save people for a living," Jared countered, frustration bubbling up. "I don't even understand how this argument started."

"I blame Zander," Harper offered helpfully. "He's been a real pill all day."

Zander was affronted. "I have not!"

"You have so," Harper shot back. "You've been giving me grief for hours about moving in with Jared. I'm sick of it."

Zander adopted a wounded expression. "I don't care if you move in with Jared. I just think I should be involved in your decorating choices."

Harper balked. "That is not what you said."

"That is exactly what I said."

"You're full of it."

Jared heaved out a sigh. "I have no idea how this conversation got so far off track. I just came over here to tell you to go home."

"It's only going to get worse when you move in together," Zander said pragmatically. "It's because the color eggplant is depressing and that's what color she wants to paint your kitchen. Do you want a depressing kitchen? I'm going to guess not."

Jared could do nothing but chuckle. "Well, I'm sure you guys will work that out. For now, I have to go back to work. You two should go home."

"Wait a second," Colin groused. "You're really moving in together? I thought Zander was making that up to irritate me. What is happening here?"

What was happening indeed?

# ❧ 3 ❧

## THREE

Jared was happy when he saw Harper and Zander pulling away from the cemetery. The medical examiner was almost finished with his initial exam and Jared was hopeful an opening to call it a night was in his immediate future. He was tired and the days running up to the Halloween holiday promised to be long with a murder to investigate. That was on top of the fact that Harper repeatedly warned him about the run-up to Halloween being her busiest time of the year. He was basically already exhausted and he'd barely started.

That didn't mean he was too tired to question his partner about Colin.

"What's the deal with the culinary kid over there?"

Mel was understandably confused because he missed the earlier conversation. "What?" He ripped his gaze away from the men packing up Maggie's body. "What culinary kid?"

"That one." Jared gestured toward Colin. "What's his deal?"

Mel's expression softened. "Oh, Colin? He's harmless."

"That's not really what I asked."

"He's extra harmless," Mel stressed. "He's one of the youngsters around here who has a chance of becoming something if he puts his mind to it. He went to college and everything."

"That's great and I don't have a problem with him going to college." Jared honestly meant it. "I wish him all the best on his financial management track. I'm more curious about his interest in Harper."

"Oh, *that*." Mel was genuinely amused. "I believe it started about the time Harper and Zander founded GHI."

Jared had never given it much thought. "How did that come about? I never really thought about it because the business seemed normal to me, but when they started it, the town must have been buzzing with talk."

"Oh, the town was buzzing with talk," Mel confirmed. "Everyone thought Harper and Zander were nuts. People were constantly laughing and talking behind their backs for weeks. It was a nightmare."

"I thought you told me people respected Harper because of her gift," Jared challenged. "That's what you told me when I first arrived and thought she was nuts."

Mel snorted at the memory, genuinely amused. "Yeah. You were so funny. You asked me if she was crazy and then proceeded to fall in love with her practically overnight even though you were convinced she needed to be fitted for a straightjacket. It was kind of cute."

Jared made a face. "I didn't think she needed to be fitted for a straightjacket." That was mostly true. "As for falling in love with her, I didn't do it at first sight."

"Uh-huh."

"It took like five minutes of looking at her." Jared smirked, amused at his memories. "Tell me about the opening of the business, though. What was up with that? And what does it have to do with Colin?"

"Listen, I don't know what to tell you about that because I tried to keep my professional interests separate from their ... um, aims ... for a long time after they opened GHI," Mel explained. "I told you before that I have trouble believing in ghosts and yet, despite that, I never doubted Harper was special, that she had a certain ability.

"When they started the business, everyone in both families tried talking them out of it," he continued. "We were all worried about people staring at Harper, pegging her as different, and maybe somehow trying to exploit her."

"What about Zander?" Jared queried. "Weren't you worried about him?"

Mel immediately started shaking his head. "Not even a little. He always loved being the center of attention. It was easy to understand why he thought GHI was a good idea. Harper was another story. She was always quiet and never wanted to talk about what she could do. Starting a business was the exact opposite of hiding her abilities so ... we were all concerned."

"It obviously worked out," Jared prodded. "How did Colin come into play? I just wanted to know when his crush on Harper started."

"That's what I'm trying to tell you. Harper and Zander ignored everyone who laughed at them when they started the business and they decided to host a walk at the cemetery — one that no one had to register for because they didn't expect more than a handful of people to show up — and Colin was one of the first ones there."

"He was a kid, though, right?"

Mel nodded. "He was eighteen but definitely a kid. He was always moony over Harper, even when he was in middle school and she was graduating high school. She was sweet to him, which probably did him a disservice because if she'd been mean he would've moved on and you wouldn't be giving him the stink eye."

"I don't want her to be mean. I just don't like the way he looks at her. She treats him like a kid, but he's technically a man."

"Ugh." Mel made a face. "I can't believe you're getting worked up over a recent college graduate when you're getting ready to move in with your girlfriend. Colin Thompson is not a threat."

"I didn't say he was a threat," Jared said. "I merely said he irritated me."

"I don't think you have anything to worry about." Mel straightened as the medical examiner's aide approached and handed him a sheet of paper. "Colin Thompson is completely harmless. So what if he has a crush on your girlfriend?"

Jared wanted to argue further, but he knew it made him look petty. "Fine. You're right. Colin Thompson is a boy and I'm a man. I should be above things like this."

"Great." Mel tapped his finger against the sheet of paper. "We have

Maggie's address and notification information. We should probably head that way. We can't do anything else until we get time of death from the medical examiner, and that won't come until tomorrow."

Jared nodded, turning serious. "Then we should do it."

**MAGGIE HARRIS WAS** a local girl, but she didn't live with her family. Her mother and father moved to Florida full time the year before and her only living grandparents were in a home two counties over. What Maggie Harris did have, though, was a roommate ... and she was utterly flabbergasted to find Jared and Mel on her front porch shortly before eleven.

"W-what are you doing here?" Heather Bancroft was in her mid-twenties – just like Maggie – and she was clearly shaken.

"Hey, Heather." Mel forced a smile as he held his hat in hand. "I don't suppose we could come in for a few minutes, could we?"

"Um, sure." Heather dubiously looked between Mel and Jared as she turned on her heel and walked into the living room, leaving Jared to shut the front door. "Is something wrong? Is it my mom?"

Mel immediately started shaking his head. "It's not your mom, Heather."

"It is someone, though, right?"

Mel nodded. There was never an easy way to break news of this sort so he decided to rip off the bandage and tell her straight away. "We found Maggie tonight. I'm sorry to inform you of this, but she's dead."

Heather's mouth dropped open as she worked her jaw, but no sound would come out. Mel decided to fill the silence with something soothing while he waited for her reaction.

"I'm sorry to have to call on you so late ... or at all ... but we have a few questions," he said.

Heather mutely nodded. "Right. Yeah. Questions." She flicked her eyes to Jared. "Are you sure it's Maggie? I mean ... you haven't been in town very long. You might have mistaken her for someone else. That happens, right?"

Jared took pity on her and decided not to take the question as an insult. "Not really. We checked her fingerprints, though. We found her purse on the scene. We're sure it's her."

"I was there, too," Mel added gently. "I saw her. I recognized her. It's definitely Maggie."

"Oh, my ... ." Heather sank into a nearby chair, her strength waning as Mel stripped away the last hope she had that everything would work out. "I don't understand how this happened. I just saw her."

"That's what we're trying to figure out." Mel settled on the couch across from Heather. "You guys worked at the bank together, right?"

Heather bobbed her head. "We knew each other from high school and were friendly but not friends. That changed when we both got jobs at the bank and decided to move in together. It just made sense from a financial standpoint. We were both trying to put money away."

"Was she troubled by anything recently?" Mel asked.

"I ... troubled? No. She was in a good mood." Heather knit her eyebrows. "Wait ... you wouldn't be here if it was an accident. Well, you might be here, but you wouldn't be asking a bunch of questions and looking the way you two look. That means something else is going on, right? You think something happened to her."

"We *know* something happened to her," Jared clarified. "That's not a question. We need information about her activities over the last few days, though. When was the last time you saw her?"

"Um ... how did she die?"

Mel smiled kindly at Heather. "We can't talk about that right now. We're waiting for confirmation from the medical examiner. We can say that however she died wasn't an accident, but that's all the detail we can share at this time. What we need from you is information about Maggie and the way she lived her life so we can find out who did this to her."

"Who did this to her?" Heather's voice sounded lifeless and dull. "I don't even know what to make of this. I keep thinking that it must be a dream and that I'm going to wake up at any second."

"I wish I could answer that question, but we don't know who did this," Jared replied. "That's why we're here. We need to know the last time you saw her."

"Yesterday." Heather's voice was hollow. "We both worked at the bank and then we came back here and got dressed for a party."

Jared leaned forward, intrigued. "What party?"

"The one out at the old Standish barn on the highway," Heather replied. "They have a costume party every year. This is the third year in a row that we've attended."

Jared looked to Mel for further information. "Do you know about that party?"

Mel nodded. "Yeah. It's a big deal for the locals. I think most people of a certain age go."

"I didn't go," Jared pointed out. "Harper and Zander didn't go."

"Harper and Zander give tours five nights a week in October," Mel reminded his partner. "They don't have time to go to a party. Everyone else over the age of twenty-one – and some who only have fake IDs – find their way there on the Friday before Halloween. It's tradition."

"So you went to the party together?" Jared prodded Heather. "Did you get separated?"

Heather shrugged. "I ... well ... I know this is going to sound bad – especially given how things turned out – but we never planned on going home together. We both were going to hook up with someone, go home with them, and then just catch up today."

"But you didn't catch up today, did you?" Mel asked.

"No, but I didn't really think much of that either," Heather admitted. "I just thought Maggie found someone she really hit it off with and I was happy for her."

"Did you see her with anyone at the party?"

"No. The minute I got there, someone put a drink in my hand and I lost sight of her. I didn't see her at all after that. I ... you don't think someone at the party did something to her, do you?"

Mel and Jared exchanged a weighted look.

"That's exactly what we're going to find out," Mel replied after a beat. "We need to know who was at that party. Tell me about everything and everyone you can remember."


**HARPER WAS ALREADY ASLEEP** when Jared let himself into

her bedroom. It was after midnight and the house was quiet when he used his key to let himself in. He was looking forward to a time when he would be able to share a roof with just her, but for tonight he was glad that she wasn't left alone to wait for him to finish work. That was one of the things he worried about most.

"Hi," Harper murmured as she shifted and cuddled against him.

"Hey, Heart." Jared kissed her forehead and wrapped his arms around her as he tucked the covers tightly around both of them. "I didn't mean to wake you. I'm sorry."

"That's okay." Harper's voice was full of sleep and Jared knew she would drift off quickly. "Did you find out anything?"

"Not a lot. We can talk about it tomorrow."

"Any suspects?"

Jared chuckled as he rubbed his hands over her slim back. "We can talk about it over breakfast."

"Okay." Harper rubbed her cheek against Jared's solid chest. "Did you make notification?"

"Yes. To her roommate. Her parents are in Florida. Mel is waiting until tomorrow morning to call them."

"That's a call no one ever wants to get."

"No one ever wants to give it either." Jared danced his fingers over Harper's back, briefly wondering if she would slip into sleep right away. He waited for a long beat and then asked the obvious question as a test. "Did you and Zander make up?"

"We weren't really fighting."

"You said he suddenly doesn't want you to move," Jared pointed out. "I want you to know that I had a very long talk with him before I even brought this up to you because I was afraid of a meltdown. He said it would be fine."

"I know." Harper wasn't bothered in the least by Zander's theatrics. "You don't have to get all worked up or anything. Don't let Zander bother you. He's just talking to hear himself talk right now."

"So ... what? Do you think he'll let this whole thing go and stop giving you grief about moving?"

"No. He's going to keep giving both of us grief for weeks after we

24

move." Harper stifled a yawn. "He can't help himself. He's opposed to change."

"You're moving across the road," Jared offered. "You won't be very far away. We need privacy, though. *I* need privacy."

"That's what I told him. Don't worry." Harper lightly tapped her fingers on Jared's chest to soothe him. "He's okay with the move. He's mad at himself because he's okay with it, but he really is okay with it."

Jared ran the convoluted logic through his head. "If he's okay with it, why did he pick a fight with you today?"

"Because he wants control of our decorating process."

"I thought that was something you and I were supposed to do together."

"It is, but Zander loves to decorate." Harper tipped her mouth up and kissed Jared's jaw. "Don't worry. It really will be okay. I know exactly how to handle Zander. I've been doing it for a very long time."

"I know." Jared involuntarily shuddered when her busy lips, which were busy close to his mouth, sent a chill down his spine. "I thought you were tired, Heart. You don't seem all that tired to me."

"I'm starting to think that the pizza gave me a second wind of sorts."

"Is that a fact?"

Harper giggled when Jared tickled her ribs and flipped her to her back in one smooth move, leaving her breathless as she widened her eyes and locked gazes with him. "I'm definitely getting a second wind."

"And here I was trying to be gentlemanly and quiet when I came in," Jared teased, nuzzling his nose against her cheek as he kissed his way around her soft skin. "I guess I just should've thrown myself on you and beat my chest like Tarzan when I came home to make you feel loved, huh?"

Harper's laugh was so sweet it warmed Jared's heart. "I like it when you pretend to be Tarzan. Definitely do that next time."

"Sure." He kissed her firmly on the mouth. "Now that I have you awake, though, I want to hear everything about the president of your fan club. I'm willing to torture you to get the information."

It took Harper a moment to realize what Jared was referring to. "You can't be serious. Colin is harmless."

"So I've heard ... repeatedly. I still like torturing you when I can do it with kisses."

Harper's eyes lit with mirth. "So ... what are you waiting for?"

"I thought you'd never ask." Jared swallowed Harper's giggles with a kiss. "Prepare yourself for some intensive interrogation, missy. I'm in charge now."

"That sounds like a fun game."

"You have no idea."

## 4

# FOUR

"Hey, Heart."

Harper woke to find Jared cuddled close, his arms wrapped around her, and a bright smile on his face. They were cocooned together under the blankets and she couldn't think of a place she would rather be.

"Hi." She sounded a bit breathless as she stretched and kissed the tip of his nose. The events of the previous evening came back to her quickly when she realized her shirt was hanging off the nearby lamp and her cheeks flushed with heat and pleasure at the memory. "I guess we didn't get dressed again before going to sleep, huh?"

Jared shook his head, genuinely amused. "Nope. Not even a little." He rubbed his nose against her cheek. "I love how warm and soft you are in the morning. Have I ever told you that?"

"Oh, and here I thought you loved everything about me."

"I do." Jared poked her taut stomach. "I especially love mornings we get to spend together, though."

"I love mornings like that, too," Harper admitted. "We still should've gotten dressed."

"And why is that?"

"Because it's Sunday."

Jared furrowed his brow. "So? Since when are you a calendar watcher?"

"Since ... ." Harper broke off and pointed toward the door, her lips curving when it popped open on cue to allow Zander entrance. He was dressed in a set of monogrammed cotton pajamas, his hair already brushed, and he made a beeline for Harper's side of the bed.

"It's starting to get cold," Zander announced, tugging at the covers even as Harper made a big show of keeping him from slipping underneath. "It will be winter before you know it. I'm so not looking forward to that."

"No one is," Harper agreed, keeping a firm grip on the blanket.

"What are you doing?" Zander slowed his efforts and frowned at his best friend. "Why are you trying to stop me from getting in bed with you? It's Sunday. I'm allowed to be here on Sundays. That's the rule."

"I know." Harper shot a pointed look to Jared. "Do you want to tell him what the big deal is?"

Since Jared was the one who instituted the rule about Zander only being allowed to visit their bed one day a week – and this was after months of fighting and grappling for control – naturally he would have to be the one to explain the problem this morning. He wasn't keen to be part of that conversation, though, so he merely shrugged. "I don't care what you tell him. Just get him out of here."

"I heard that." Zander stopped his manic cover manipulation. "I don't really care what you do or don't like this morning. This is my Harper time and you don't need to be here."

Jared narrowed his eyes. "Excuse me? You have been with Harper almost fifteen hours a day for two weeks straight. I barely get to see her. I don't think you want to start comparing who misses her more."

"Oh, whatever." Zander theatrically rolled his eyes. "You said I could only visit on Sundays so here I am. You can't change the rules now."

"I believe my initial rule was that you could only visit once a week on work days," Jared grumbled. "You whined so hard and so long about that rule I finally had to give in and give you Sundays, even though that's one of the few days Harper and I often have off together."

"All I hear when you whine like that is 'blah, blah, blah,'" Zander deadpanned. "Now let me under the covers. It's cold. I don't like being cold."

Zander had seen her naked enough times Harper didn't have a problem with it happening again. She knew Jared was another story, though, and she didn't want to start their lazy Sunday morning together with a meltdown.

"Zander, I think we should postpone our morning ritual until tomorrow," Harper hedged.

"What? No!" Zander was agitated. "I don't want to postpone it. I've been dreaming of this meeting of the design minds since last Sunday morning. I even brought a catalog." He held up a Restoration Hardware catalog for emphasis. "Now, let me in!"

"Oh, geez." Jared pinched the bridge of his nose. "I can't wait until we have our own place and can wake up alone every Sunday morning."

"As you like to continuously point out, it's right across the road and five hundred yards isn't going to stop me from visiting Harper when I need a fix of my favorite person in the world," Zander sneered.

"Well, at least I know where I land in the pecking order," Shawn Donovan deadpanned as he appeared in the open doorway. Unlike his boyfriend, Shawn's hair was a mess and he wore simple jogging pants and a T-shirt to sleep in rather than Zander's fussy monogrammed offerings. "I always knew I ranked behind Harper, but it's good I've finally heard it with my own ears."

Zander balked. "Oh, that's not true. You know I love you. It's just … it's Sunday. Harper and I are supposed to spend Sundays together."

"You've spent the past two weeks together," Jared barked, refusing to release Harper from his grip even as she squirmed to prop herself in an effort to meet Zander's accusatory gaze. "We've barely seen each other during that time."

"And whose fault is that?"

Jared was incensed. "Yours! You guys give ghost tours constantly and because of your increased schedule I never get to see my girlfriend."

"Yes, well, I think that's a lesson in karma for you." Zander studied his fingernail beds for a moment and then gave the covers another vicious yank with his other hand. "Let me in!"

Shawn widened his eyes to comical proportions at Zander's reaction. He was used to his boyfriend's dramatic ways but occasionally there were times when Zander could still surprise him. "Stop yelling at them," Shawn instructed, his voice calm and even. "They clearly don't want you in here this morning. Stop bugging them."

"You stop bugging me," Zander fired back. "This is my ritual with Harper. We've always done this. I don't want it to stop even though Jared is stealing her from me."

"Ugh. Here we go." Jared slapped his hand to his forehead. "I just can't deal with the drama this morning. Do you have any idea how tired I am? This is my only day off this week. We had a murder last night and the only reason I still have today off is because the medical examiner's office is behind and we can't do anything until we have a time of death to work with. So just ... shut up."

"Shut up?" Zander's eyebrows practically jumped off his forehead. "Shut up? Did you just tell me to shut up?" He turned to Shawn for confirmation. "Did he just tell me to shut up?"

"I think that was the general gist," Shawn replied dryly, reaching over and lifting Harper's discarded camisole top from the nearby lamp. Realization dawned on his face and he had to bite his lip to keep from laughing. "I think, just this once, you should probably leave them to their Sunday morning routine and come with me to the kitchen."

"What?" Zander was furious. "This is my time!"

Shawn held up the camisole. "I think they had their own brand of special time last night and that's why they don't want you under the covers with them."

Zander snatched the camisole and stared at it for a long beat. "Oh. Is that it?"

Harper pressed her lips together and nodded. "I'm sorry. We'll make up for it next weekend, though. I promise."

"I don't care if you're naked." Zander turned pragmatic. "I don't even like your parts so it's not a big deal."

"I think it's a big deal today," Harper said, making a face when Jared clutched her tighter. "We'll make up for it next weekend. I swear it. I'll even kick Jared out of bed so it's just you and me."

"Ugh." Jared buried his face in Harper's hair.

Zander brightened considerably. "Fine. I want brunch, though, too."

Harper nodded without hesitation. "I'm looking forward to it."

Zander turned to stomp out of the room, every intention of slamming the bedroom door shut for good measure written across his face, but Jared stopped him when he reached out and grabbed the catalog before Zander could breeze by.

"We'll take this. Thanks." Jared's smile was so smarmy it set Zander's teeth on edge. "We planned to go furniture shopping this afternoon anyway. This is a great way to start."

Zander was horrified. "You can't go furniture shopping without me!"

"Oh, it's going to happen." Jared turned smug as he flipped over the catalog and studied the cover. "Reclaimed wood. Nice. I'm going to love checking out this place."

Zander turned to Shawn, helplessness lighting his handsome features. "This is pure torture."

Shawn sympathetically patted his arm. "You're okay. We'll spend the day together and you'll be fine."

"I don't think I'll ever be fine again." Zander was morose as Shawn tugged him through the door. "I might need a pedicure to perk me up."

Shawn smiled. "I think that sounds like a fabulous idea."


**TWO HOURS LATER,** Jared and Harper were showered, dressed, and fed. They were also at the Restoration Hardware furniture store and having a grand time looking at all the shopping options.

"This is nice." Jared bounced up and down on a reclaimed wood bed and admired the rustic look of the furniture. "I know I should hate this stuff on principle because Zander picked it out, but I like wood like this. It's attractive and homey. I think we should definitely consider it for our new place."

Harper smiled as she studied the price tag on the furniture. "It's kind of expensive."

Jared turned serious as he shifted his eyes to her. "Don't worry about that. I've got some money put away and you're going to have some money when Shawn pays you for your half of the current house."

"I know but ... I want to give you all that money for the new house," Harper reminded him. "We're sharing expenses so that means I have to pay for half."

Jared studied her for a long beat. "Well, not necessarily." He licked his lips, uncertain how to proceed. This was a sticky area he hadn't considered when he suggested moving in together. "I technically paid the down payment on the house and we already closed on it. Your name is on everything so ... it's fine."

"You paid the down payment with the agreement that I would give you money once Shawn bought me out of my half of the house I share with Zander," Harper clarified. "I'm going to give you that money as soon as I get it."

"Or you could spend it on furniture." Jared petted the bed and offered a charming grin. "I'm a big fan of reclaimed wood, in case you haven't noticed. I love this store and I'm thinking we need this bed."

Harper was less convinced. "Maybe we should save our money for a year and then buy furniture once we're on firmer financial ground. I'm sure we can muddle through with what we have until then. We don't necessarily need a bed because I already have one."

"Yes, and as much as I love particle board furniture, I thought we would go nuts and buy something nicer," Jared pressed. "What's really going on here?" He sensed trouble. "Are you changing your mind about us moving in together?"

The question caught Harper off guard. "Of course not!" She didn't mean to screech, but she couldn't stop herself. "This is what I want more than anything. You should know that. The thing is, I want to do this the right way. I mean ... you shouldn't pay for the house and then put my name on it as if I somehow paid as much as you. That doesn't seem fair."

Jared narrowed his eyes, confused. "I really don't want this to turn into a thing so I need you to tell me what's going through that head of yours. You're starting to worry me."

Harper balked. "I don't want to worry you. I simply want things to be fair."

"And you think they're not fair, right?"

"I think that you put twenty thousand dollars of your own money down to buy us a house and then listed both of our names on the documents at closing," Harper replied. "I haven't given you any money yet. How do you know I'm going to?"

Jared held his hands palms out and shrugged. "Intuition? Let's just say I think you're a good bet."

Harper made a face. "And what if I'm a grifter?"

Jared found the notion so surreal he could do nothing but chuckle. "Are you a grifter?"

"No, but I could be."

"You're not, though." Jared ran his tongue over his teeth as he collected Harper's hand and tugged hard enough that she had no choice but to sit down next to him. "I think we should start from the beginning because you seem a little manic, my love, and I don't like it when you're manic. This is supposed to be fun. We're plotting our life together ... and starting with furniture. What's more fun than that?"

"It *is* going to be fun," Harper agreed. "Once I pay you back the money I owe you it's going to be a lot of fun."

"Uh-huh." Jared wasn't convinced. "How much money do you think you owe me?"

"Twenty thousand dollars."

"And why do you feel you owe me that?"

"Because that's how much you spent on the house," Harper replied without hesitation. "This is a partnership. It can't be you spending money and me accepting that sort of imbalance because then that's not a partnership. Then that's you taking care of me."

"And just so I'm clear, you don't want me taking care of you, right?"

"I want us to take care of each other," Harper clarified. "I don't want to feel that you're doing everything and I'm doing nothing, though. I can't wait to move in together, but I want to feel as if I'm contributing."

"Okay." Jared patted her hand. "I want you to contribute, too. I think this is going to be a good thing for both of us. I didn't realize you were so worked up about the idea of owing me money, though. I guess I should've taken that into account. I didn't want to wait until you had the money from selling your share of the house to Shawn, though, because I was afraid someone else would swoop in and steal our house."

"And I wouldn't want to risk waiting on that either," Harper admitted. "I just want to give you twenty thousand dollars so I don't feel as if you've given everything to this partnership and I've given nothing."

Jared wasn't sure he completely understood but he was starting to get a picture. "We've done the math a few times. You should end up with about forty thousand dollars once you close on your house. You want to give twenty thousand of that to me so we can apply it to the mortgage on the new house, right?"

Harper nodded. "Then we'll both split everything down the middle going forward for payments and furniture. That's the only fair thing."

Jared thought that sounded a bit ridiculous, but he decided now wasn't the time to pick a fight. "You're still going to have money, though, and I'm going to have money, too. I don't understand why we can't buy a bed."

"Because we're going to need to use that money for appliances and workers to paint and do things around the house. I didn't say we couldn't buy a bed. I just think we should do the other stuff first."

"The appliances are out of date and so are the cupboards," Jared agreed. "I don't think it's going to cost as much as you think to replace some of that stuff, though, especially if we're splitting costs."

"I just want to be sure." Harper turned earnest. "This is a big deal for me. When Zander and I first moved in together I always thought it was going to be a temporary thing and then it turned kind of permanent. This is a big change."

Jared smirked. "It is a big change. I've never lived with anyone before. Er, well, I lived with a bunch of guys while attending the police academy, but you know what I mean."

"I do. We're taking two lives and making one."

Jared tilted his head to the side and made a face. "Not exactly.

We're taking two lives and interlocking them." He lifted their joined fingers for emphasis. "We've already got a good start on it. I think it's going to be easier than you happen to believe."

"I think it's going to be great." Harper was honest and earnest. "I still want to pay for the necessities before we start thinking about beds. Besides, this is my busy month. By the end of the month I might have even more money to throw at a bed."

Even though he didn't fully understand Harper's need to keep a balanced ledger book, Jared offered a wry smile. "Then let's head to lunch and do the practical thing."

"What's the practical thing?"

"Break down all of our finances and figure out what's going to work for both of us."

Harper brightened considerably. "You would really do that?"

"I would do anything for you."

"And that's why you're the perfect guy."

Jared grinned and pressed a quick kiss against her mouth. "I couldn't agree more. Come on. I'm starving and there's nothing that screams 'lazy Sunday afternoon' like figuring out finances."

"I know you're being sarcastic, but I'm looking forward to this."

Jared chuckled. "That's only one of the reasons I love you."

## 5

## FIVE

Jared picked a corner booth at the restaurant and was amused when Harper happily pulled out a notebook and began scribbling away mere seconds after the waitress left with their dinner orders. He had no idea why she was so excited to budget, but he was content to let her throw numbers at him to her heart's content.

"So, once we have the total forty thousand down, our house payments are going to be less than five hundred a month," Harper started. "I think we should make double payments because then we'll own the house outright in a few years. I can even pay more once October is over because of all the extra money I'm bringing in this month."

"No way." Jared made a tsking sound with his tongue as he wagged his finger. "You're not paying extra. You just had a fit because you didn't like it when it seemed like I was paying extra. We're doing everything right down the middle."

Harper made a face. "Fine. It was just a suggestion."

"Well, you can't have it your way if I can't have it my way." Jared played with his straw wrapper. "I'm fine paying double every month. That's going to be the same as what I'm currently paying in rent for a house I'm never at."

"Speaking of that, when is your lease up?" Harper asked.

"Technically not for another five months, but I talked to the land-lord and he agreed to allow Jeff to take over the payments. He's been living there and taking care of the place anyway and he's managed to save up enough for first and last month's rent so it should be fine."

Harper offered a genuine smile. Jeff Clarke was a homeless man she found months before and Jared adopted out of a desire to help. He put up the guy in the apartment above his garage, got him started mowing lawns and eventually clearing snow, and helped him get on his feet. She was proud Jared managed to help Jeff build a home ... mostly because she didn't know a lot of people who would be that giving of their time and assets. "That's nice. Is Jeff upset that you're moving?"

"He said that he's surprised it didn't happen sooner because we're joined at the hip."

Harper snickered. "That sounds like him. We should make sure we still make time to hang out with him when we can, make sure he doesn't think we've forgotten him or something."

"That's a plan." Jared bobbed his head. "I do need to run out to that place and grab the rest of my stuff by the end of the week, though. I'm officially off the lease as of November. I don't think Jeff should have to store my stuff because I'm too lazy to pick it up."

"We'll make sure to pick it up." Harper cocked her head to the side as she considered the change. "When can we move into the new house?"

"We could do it today if you wanted." Jared's grin was slow and easy. "There's still some work that needs to be done over there, but if you don't mind living in a mess we can start packing right now. I will personally move all of your things by myself if it means not having to deal with Zander in the morning tomorrow."

Harper frowned. "He's not so bad."

Jared silently cursed himself for not thinking before he spoke. "That's not what I meant and you know it. I happen to – well, 'love' isn't the right word, but 'like' will work – I happen to like Zander, too. He's simply a lot to deal with day in and day out."

"He's just the emotional sort. He can't help himself."

"I get that. No, I really do." Jared smiled brightly. "He's still nuttier than a Snickers left out in the sun to melt."

Harper pressed her lips together to keep from laughing. "He just wants to be included in the process."

"We have included him. His problem is that he wants to take over everything."

"Not everything."

Jared made a face. "What hasn't he tried to take over?"

"Well ... he hasn't made a fuss about changing out the appliances yet. That's something."

"Does he know we're changing out the appliances?"

"What does that have to do with anything?"

"Just give him time." Despite his irritation, Jared couldn't stop himself from being amused. "The original plan was to be in the new house by Christmas. Do you want to try and move that up?"

"No." Harper shook her head. "I'm surprised you actually managed to get a closing date so fast. How did you work that out, by the way?"

"A man was murdered in that house," Jared reminded her. "His daughter wanted to unload it as quickly as possible. She was highly motivated."

"Good point." Harper's grin was serene as she leaned back in her seat. "When are the people coming in to get all of Henry's belongings out of the house?"

"Next week."

"And then we have cleaners coming, right?"

Jared bobbed his head. "I hired people out of Troy. They will take a full two days to do absolutely everything, including walls and windows, and then we have some decisions to make."

"Appliances and paint colors."

"Yes. You mentioned wanting to hire professionals to paint, which I'm fine with, but then we need to pick colors."

"You act as if we have a choice in the matter," Harper countered. "Can you paint?"

"Yes. Can't you?"

Harper immediately started shaking her head. "I honestly paint like a five-year-old with finger paints and a coloring book. Can you paint well?"

"I believe I can do everything well." Jared shot her a hot look. "And I do mean *everything*."

"Ha, ha." Even though she knew he was teasing, Harper felt her cheeks flush with burning color. "What were we talking about again?"

Jared snickered, amused by her discomfort. "We were talking about painting. If you want to save money so we can buy that bed I love, here's a way to do it. I'm very good at painting. In fact, I did it for a company four years running during summers when I was in college."

Harper was pleasantly surprised. "And you can really do it as good as a professional?"

Jared's wolfish smile was back. "I can do everything as well as a professional."

"Okay, knock it off with the sexy talk." Harper sipped her iced tea. "If you can really paint, that would save us thousands of dollars."

"I can really paint."

"I might need to see examples of your work to be sure."

Jared poked her side. "Do you want references, too?"

"Only from your painting work. If you have references from the other work you're bragging about I don't want to talk to those people. In fact, I like to pretend those people don't exist."

"Very cute. As for the painting. I can do it. Pick your colors and I can have it done in a reasonable timeframe."

"Well, that's something to celebrate right there."

"You have no idea how excited I am to hear that. I think I know how we can celebrate and everything."

"Somehow that doesn't surprise me."

**HARPER AND JARED ENJOYED** an easy and cozy dinner, taking advantage of their time together to flip through the catalog and point out things they both liked. If Jared had his druthers they would use Harper's money to buy furniture and take longer to pay off the house, but she was adamant that paying off the house should be their first priority.

"It's fun to look at this stuff, but we need to get inside the house and measure the space," Harper noted. "I barely managed to make it to the closing on time because of all the tours. We haven't even measured our space and taken a hard look at our furniture needs."

Jared pursed his lips as he wiped the corners of his mouth. "Well, what stuff do you own in the current house?"

"My bed and dresser."

"That's it?"

Harper nodded. "Zander has a thing about furniture. He insisted on buying most of it because he wanted the final say in every decision. I let him do it because it was easier than arguing."

"I wish I could even feign surprise, but I can't," Jared said, sliding his arm around Harper's shoulders as he got comfortable. "So, you're basically saying that we have a bed and a dresser, huh?"

"That's what I have," Harper countered.

"Then that's what *we* have." Jared's smile was rueful.

Harper wasn't sure what to make of the news. "You're like thirty-one."

"Thirty," Jared corrected, extending a finger. "I have four months before I'm thirty-one. Let's not rush things."

Harper held her hands up in a placating manner. "I'm sorry. I didn't realize you were phobic about getting old. That's something I'm going to have to file away and think about later."

"I'm not phobic about getting old," Jared clarified. "I just like being thirty. I don't want to be thirty-one."

"Of course." Harper bit back a smile. "Still, though, you're thirty and have no furniture. How did that happen?"

"It's not as big a deal as you make it out to be. I simply rented my whole life – and that includes furniture – so I have absolutely nothing to offer the new house when it comes to furniture."

"Huh." Harper was flummoxed. "I thought for sure you would have a kitchen table or something. We can't make it with just a bed."

"Well, we could."

Harper lightly slapped Jared's arm, but it didn't dislodge the smile on his face. "We might have to buy a few pieces of furniture early after all."

"My bed." Jared eagerly rubbed his hands together.

"We have a bed."

"I want a new bed. I want us to have something that belongs to us and no one else ever slept in ... including Zander. I'm not going to change my mind on that."

"Fine. We'll get a new bed."

"Great." Jared brightened, his smile widening until he caught sight of a familiar face approaching the table. "Oh, you've got to be kidding me. I thought we were finally going to talk about something I wanted to talk about."

Harper squinched her face and frowned, confused. "What are you complaining about?"

"Hey, Harper! It's so good to see you."

Harper practically jumped out of her skin when Colin appeared on the other side of the booth seat and poked his head between her and Jared. "Colin," she rasped out, her heart pounding. "I didn't see you there."

"I can't believe I didn't see you either." Colin barreled forward, clearly oblivious to Harper's discomfort. "We've been here for almost an hour and I only saw you when I was coming back from the bathroom – the refried beans from the fajitas went right through me, I swear. I wish I would've seen you sooner because then we could've eaten together."

"Yes, that would've been delightful," Jared drawled.

His response was enough to calm Harper and cause her to shoot him a warning look. While she fully understood Colin wore on Jared's last nerve, there was no way she would allow her boyfriend to mistreat the gregarious young man. He really was harmless and his crush was cute ... at least to Harper.

"I'm sorry we didn't get a chance to talk to you earlier, too," Harper said smoothly. "Who are you here with?"

"Oh, some guys I graduated with." Colin pointed toward a table in the corner and Harper recognized most of the faces when she caught sight of them.

"That's Rick Derry, Jay Forrester, Sam Archer and Dean Collins, right?"

Colin nodded. "This is the first time we've been able to hang out together since graduating from high school. Rick and Sam live on the west side of the state now but came home for the weekend barn party – you know how that is – and Dean lives over in Utica. Jay is still with his folks. We've been having a good time hanging out, though."

Harper grinned. "I forgot all about the barn party."

Mention of the party jostled something in Jared's mind. He'd almost forgotten what Heather told him about Maggie's last known whereabouts – or at least dislodged the information until he returned to work the next day – but Colin's simple statement brought him back to reality.

"That's the same party that Maggie Harris was at right before she disappeared," Jared noted. "Did you see her there?"

"Who are you talking about?" Colin looked confused.

"She works at the bank," Harper supplied. "She was two years ahead of you in school." She turned to Jared, conflicted. "You didn't tell me that Maggie was at the annual barn party before going missing."

"I didn't think much about it," Jared admitted. "I found out from Maggie's roommate – a woman named Heather Bancroft – that they went to the party together but left separately."

Harper wrinkled her forehead. "Why would they leave separately? That doesn't sound like very smart party behavior. Zander and I always made it a rule to stick together at parties so no one could separate us. Zander was very worried about someone trying to roofie his drink."

"Yes, well, I don't think you and Zander were going to parties for the same reason that Heather and Maggie were going to parties," Jared supplied.

"I ... don't understand."

"He's saying they went to the party to hook up," Colin interjected helpfully. "I know the girls you're talking about. I didn't immediately recognize the last names, but I knew them from the bank. They were definitely at the barn party."

"You saw them there?" Jared leaned forward. "How come you didn't mention that when we were at the cemetery last night?"

Colin shrugged. "Why would I mention it?"

"Because you saw the dead girl the night before she was murdered and dumped in the cemetery. Are you saying you didn't think that was important?"

"Jared," Harper scolded. "Don't be mean to him."

Jared ignored Harper's admonishment. "I'm just trying to understand why he didn't say anything."

"I didn't say anything because I didn't realize who it was," Colin explained. "I didn't look at the body at the cemetery because ... well ... it was ... um ... ."

Harper sympathetically patted Colin's arm. "It's okay. It was traumatic for all of us. There's nothing to be ashamed about. I didn't want to look either."

"I don't think he believes there's nothing to be ashamed about." Colin jerked his chin in Jared's direction, his dislike for the police officer obvious. "He thinks I was a baby not to look."

Jared would never use the word "baby" as an insult – at least on purpose – but he had trouble disagreeing with the sentiment. Still, the look on Harper's face told him it would be a bad idea to push things too far. She felt protective of Colin for some reason, even though he was a grown man who kept panting after Jared's girlfriend.

"I understand not looking at a body." Jared chose his words carefully. "I have to look because it's my job. If it wasn't my job, I wouldn't look."

"Because it's gross and icky?" Colin asked.

"Because it's ... both of those things." Jared avoided Harper's mirth-filled eyes. "No one is judging you for not looking."

"Good." Colin exhaled heavily and briefly allowed his adoring gaze to trace Harper's high cheekbones before dragging his eyes to an annoyed looking Jared. "What were we talking about again?"

"Maggie Harris," Jared replied, tugging on his fraying patience. He was at his limit with Colin and his antics. "You said she was at the barn party the night before the cemetery tour. She died between the time she arrived there and the time you guys found her at the end of the tour so ... what was she doing at the party?"

"Oh, well, I don't know." Colin screwed up his face into a thoughtful expression. "I guess I saw her with a group of guys near the bar."

"What bar?" Jared was behind the curve. "I thought you said the party was in a barn."

"It is in a barn," Harper explained. "This party has been going on for years, though. I mean like ... years. It was around when I was in high school. Every year a group of people gets together to organize it – it's not always the same group – and the organizers have gotten pretty good at filling the place with a lot of bodies. Three years ago, they built a bar out there and everything to add to the ambiance. It's nice."

Jared was dumbfounded. "I thought this was an abandoned barn."

"It is. People enjoy the party, though, and you can't have a good party without a bar."

"Wow." Every time Jared thought he got a handle on the weird hijinks of Whisper Cove he realized he was barely scratching the surface. "I guess I'm going to need to head out to this barn tomorrow."

"Yeah. It couldn't hurt." Harper flicked her eyes to Colin and didn't miss the dark look he shot Jared when he thought no one was looking. She snapped her fingers to drag Colin's eyes to her. "Hey. What else do you know about Maggie Harris?"

Colin shrugged. "I just know that people were saying she was easy and if I wanted a date that night to look no further than her. I don't like my women easy, though. I like them difficult ... with blonde hair and blue eyes and laughter that sounds like fairies in a garden." Colin realized what he said too late to take it back. "I mean ... I like them pretty and complicated and able to see ghosts."

Jared made a sound as he shook his head. "I'm betting that sounded better in your head, huh, kid?"

Colin drew his eyebrows together. "I don't see how you lucked out and got her. I really don't."

Jared's smile was easy. "That makes two of us. I guess I'm just lucky."

"Yeah, yeah." Colin focused on Harper. "Are you sure you want to live with this guy? I won't always live in my mother's basement."

Harper took pity on Colin and ruffled his hair. "You'll make a fine catch for some woman one day. I'm looking forward to seeing that happening."

Jared tilted his head so he could lean closer to Colin. "She's basically telling you to move on, sport."

"I can't even hear you," Colin grumbled. "You're just dust in the wind."

Jared snorted. "I guess you're kind of funny. That makes me feel a little better."

## 6

# SIX

Zander was still grumpy when Jared offered him a mock salute and slipped through the front door the following morning. It was early, but Jared was keen to get back to investigating Maggie Harris' death and that meant heading out to the barn to start his day.

As for Zander and Harper, they had their own business to tend to.

"We have more than ten messages from people asking to be added to tonight's tour," Zander announced as he collected the breakfast dishes and carried them to the dishwasher. "For the record, I checked with Uncle Mel and he says we're not allowed in the cemetery tonight. That means we're going to have to postpone tonight's tour until tomorrow so we might want to allow the add-ons."

"Is that normal?" Shawn asked, cupping his coffee mug and leaning back in his chair. "I mean ... do you deal with last-second changes like that all the time?"

"We usually get an addition or a subtraction – sometimes a whole family or group – but ten calls is a bit much," Harper replied, thoughtfully narrowing her eyes. "Any idea why we have so many additions, Zander?"

Zander bobbed his head, taking Harper by surprise. "I know. You do, too, if you really think about it."

Harper tilted her head to the side, considering. It didn't take long for her to realize what her best friend was referring to. "Maggie. Everyone thinks finding her body was part of the show and they want to be involved in the investigation into her death."

"Ding, ding, ding! And we have a winner!" Zander's distaste for the conversational turn was obvious. "It's basically a bunch of ghouls who want to invite themselves along for the ride."

"Wait ... ." Shawn furrowed his brow. "Are you saying people want to be part of the next tour because they think there's a chance Harper will cross paths with Maggie and they want dirt on how she died?"

Zander nodded. "That's exactly what I'm saying."

"But ... that's horrible. Why would people do that?"

Instead of being irritated − or short-tempered − Zander merely offered his boyfriend a fond smile. "You're so pretty." He turned to Harper for backup. "Don't you think he's pretty?"

Harper didn't want to grin at Shawn's expense, but she couldn't stop herself. "He's lovely."

"Oh, stop talking down to me." Shawn wrinkled his nose. "I just don't understand why people would possibly want to insert themselves in the investigation like that ... or even participate in a tour simply because you guys discovered a body two nights ago. It makes me uncomfortable."

"It's pretty much normal." Harper drained the rest of her coffee and then stood. "Speaking of that, though, I'm going to hop into the shower and head over to the cemetery. I want to see if I can find Maggie's ghost and have a talk with her before we get kicked out of the cemetery by the cops and state police tech team."

Zander nodded. "I figured. What do you want me to do about all the calls?"

Harper ran her tongue over her lips as she considered the question. "Let them join."

"Really?" Zander was understandably dubious. "You wouldn't have allowed that in years past. How come you're allowing it this year?"

"Because Jared and I just figured out last night that the only furniture we have is my bed – which he wants to replace – so that means we need money and this is an easy way to get it," Harper replied. "They just want a show. I always put on a good show."

"Okay." Zander kept his smile in place as he watched her go, waiting until she was out of earshot to speak again. "This isn't going to end well."

"I'm sure she'll be fine," Shawn said dryly. "You don't have to worry about her. She's a big girl."

"I knew her moving away from me was going to be a bad idea."

Shawn rolled his eyes. "You're just saying that because she wants to make her own decisions on décor."

"Well ... that's my area of expertise. I should be in the thick of things, not sidelined like some talentless interior design loser."

Shawn snorted, genuinely amused. "I think you'll survive. More importantly, I happen to believe this is good for her and Jared. It's something they should be doing together. It's a couple thing. You should be happy for them."

Zander was affronted. "Sometimes I don't understand how we even ended up together. It's as if you don't get me at all."

"Yeah, yeah, yeah."


**JARED WAS ALL BUSINESS** when Mel parked in front of the party barn an hour later. He'd passed the structure numerous times since moving to Whisper Cove, but he'd never had occasion to give it much attention or thought.

"So ... what's the deal with this place again?"

Mel chuckled at his partner's obvious confusion. "It's the Standish barn. It's been here since ... well ... since I was a teenager."

Jared made a face as he studied the barn's weathered walls before flicking his eyes to the tall grass on either side of the pathway they walked. "And who owns this property?"

"Technically the bank owns this property."

"And yet it's a party house."

"It's a party barn," Mel corrected. "No one lives here."

"Oh, well, that makes it so much better," Jared drawled, dropping to his knees so he could study the trampled grass to his right. "Someone has definitely been out here. I wonder if we should call the state police and have them get an evidence team to grid the grounds."

"I think that would be a tremendous waste of time," Mel countered.

"And why is that?"

"I think you should see inside before I answer that question. You'll probably understand the situation better if you look inside first."

"Fine." Jared hated it when Mel acted as if he knew something the younger police officer couldn't possibly grasp. He scuffed his feet against the packed earth of the trail as he followed Mel to the big barn door. "I don't see why we can't just call the state police and have them give this place a good once over. It probably wouldn't even take that long."

"I'll show you exactly why not." Mel grunted as he tugged on the door and pulled it open, the bright sunshine flooding the large space with enough light that Jared could poke his head inside and immediately see why Mel thought bringing the state police into the investigation was a bad idea. "Now do you see?"

Jared groaned when he realized what they were dealing with. The barn was littered with discarded plastic cups and trash, the entire two-story structure serving as a smorgasbord of possible clues and red herrings. "Oh."

"Yeah. Now you see." Mel smirked. "This place is full of DNA – probably some we don't want to think about how it got here – and other stuff."

"Like condoms." Jared made a face as he pointed toward what was clearly a used condom on the ground. "This place is disgusting."

"It's definitely disgusting," Mel agreed as he slowly began walking through the barn. "We need to get the organizers out here to get this place cleaned up. They can't leave it like this."

Jared was back to being confused. "I don't think I understand what you're saying. Why would people come back and clean?"

"Because that's part of the rules for using this place."

"It's abandoned, though."

"Yes, but there are still rules." Mel met Jared's curious gaze and heaved out a sigh. "Like I said, the annual Halloween party has been going on for a very long time. Every year a group of kids – I call them kids, but they're actually young twenty-somethings – decide to be the ones to organize the party.

"As part of the deal – which is unsaid, but everyone manages to follow the rules – the kids are responsible for cleanup before and after the party," he continues. "They have to be diligent about the trash, too, because otherwise this place will become infested with scavengers."

"You're talking like rats and stuff, aren't you?" Jared grimaced as he darted his gaze into the corners of the barn. "Great. Now I won't be able to get the idea that rats are running around out of my head."

"That's because you're kind of a little girl at times," Mel teased. "As for evidence, I'm not sure what we can expect to find here. Maggie was strangled, not stabbed, so isolating DNA evidence we're sure is from her is going to be downright impossible."

"We should still look around in case anything stands out."

"We definitely should," Mel agreed. "There's no time like the present to start. I'll hit the main floor and you head upstairs."

Jared swallowed hard and eyed the dusty second floor with overt distaste. "Why do I have to handle the second floor?"

"You're younger and I'm the boss."

"You just don't want to go up there."

"Which is why, as your superior, I'm ordering you to do it."

"Ugh." Jared was disgusted as he picked his way through the barn. "I already know I'm going to hate this."

"At least you're in a good mental place," Mel said brightly. "Just make sure you watch where you step."

"Oh, gross. There's a cheeseburger on the floor over here."

"It could be worse. Trust me."


**"I DON'T THINK** you're listening to me."

Zander was irritated at being back at the cemetery so early in the morning – especially when the grass was frosted over and his fingers cold – and he was in the mood to take it out on Harper.

"I'm listening to you," Harper shot back, refusing to meet her friend's even gaze as she stared at the police tape that marked off the area where Maggie's body was found. "I just don't happen to agree with you."

"I think that's your biggest problem in life," Zander groused. "You don't listen to me as much as you're supposed to. It's frustrating and leads to issues."

Harper stilled long enough to glance over her shoulder. "What issues are you referring to? I don't have any issues."

"Oh, you have issues." Zander scuffed the soles of his shoes over the cobblestone walk. "I'm talking about painting your kitchen pink. I know you think it's a bad idea – probably because Jared fancies himself too manly for a nice salmon color that will warm the cockles of his cold heart – but I think you should consider it."

Harper narrowed her eyes until they were nothing but glittery blue slits. "Have you ever considered that you're a complete and total pain in the posterior when you want to be?"

Zander wasn't bothered in the least by the comment. "Pink is going to be huge on those home improvement shows in the near future. Just you wait. It will be already too late for you by then because you'll have picked a stupid color like custard or banana, but I'll remember ... which essentially means I won't let you forget this moment."

"Oh, whatever." Harper was tired of talking about interior design. "I was thinking of going with blue."

"Blue?" Zander was incredulous. "Do you want to be depressed?"

"Obviously so since I brought you to the cemetery with me," Harper grumbled as she moved away from the spot where Maddie's body was discovered and fixed her attention on the mausoleum across the way. She was immediately caught off guard when she read the name on the building out of habit. "Huh."

Sensing a change in her demeanor, Zander shifted so he was facing his best friend. "What are you 'huh-ing' about?"

Harper pointed at the mausoleum. "That."

"What about it?"

"Read the name on the top."

"Ezra Standish."

Harper waited for Zander to put it all together.

"I don't see why that's important," Zander said finally. "Is it because it's a biblical name?"

"Oh, geez." Harper slapped her hand to her forehead. "You really are slow sometimes. Ezra Standish is the former owner of the Standish barn, which just so happens to be the last place Maggie Harris was seen alive."

"Oh." Zander furrowed his brow and cuffed the back of Harper's head when she walked in front of him. "Don't ever call me 'slow.' I'm fast like lightning."

Harper snorted as she kept going in the direction of the mausoleum. "Yes, you're the Pink Lightning. That's your new super-hero name."

"I like it." Zander followed Harper, peeling off so he could look through the mausoleum window before fixing her with a curious stare. "Do you think that it's something other than a coincidence that Maggie's body was found close to the Standish mausoleum? If so, I'm going to be honest even though you probably don't want to hear it. I think you're reaching. Ezra Standish has been gone since before we were even born."

"I know." Harper thoughtfully tapped her bottom lip. "It seems too weird to be a coincidence, though. I mean ... what are the odds?"

"I think you're grasping."

"No, I really want to know what the odds are," Harper pressed. "You're good with numbers. What are the odds it was a coincidence?"

"I honestly don't know," Zander replied after a beat. "It would take me some time to figure it out. I'm willing to do that for you, though, if you're willing to consider pink for your kitchen."

Harper let loose a face that even a best friend couldn't love. "I will never paint my kitchen pink. You know I don't like the color pink."

"Only because I made that joke about you looking like Princess Hubba-Bubba when we were teenagers and you tried on the pink prom dress. I think you should be over that by now."

Harper pointed her finger at Zander, her expression dark. "You agreed never to bring up that dress again. We were going to take that image to the grave with us."

"Well, I forgot we made that agreement. That doesn't really matter, though. That is not the pink I was talking about. I was suggesting something with a hint of peach to it, something that literally makes you smile when you see it."

"McDonald's breakfast sandwiches make me smile when I see them, but I'm not going to paint my kitchen the color of Ronald McDonald's hair either."

"Just ... consider it."

Harper wanted to wrestle Zander down and put a handful of dirt in his face, but she refrained ... mostly because she knew she would never hear the end of it if she got dirt on his favorite pair of jeans. "No. Pink is off the table. You consider blue."

"I don't like blue."

"Since when?"

"Since I decided pink was the color your new kitchen wants to be," Zander replied without hesitation. "I'm not joking, Harp. I can hear spaces inside homes speak and your kitchen is one of those spaces. It wants to be pink."

"Oh, whatever." Harper didn't bother to hide her eye roll as she licked her lips and stared at the mausoleum. "Maybe we're going about this the wrong way." She decided the only way to escape the kitchen conversation was to force Zander to focus on something new. "I think we need to try something different."

"I agree." Zander was solemn. "You're finally seeing things my way. I can't tell you how relieved I am about that. Let's go to Home Depot right now."

Harper scowled. "Not that, you ninny!" She lightly smacked the back of his head. "I'm talking about Maggie Harris. You remember the woman who was murdered, right? Her needs are a lot more important than our needs right now."

"You can't live your life for others ... even if those 'others' are dead."

Harper made a gagging sound in the back of her throat. "I hate it when you decide to be a fortune cookie out of nowhere."

"As if I would ever be some random fortune cookie." Zander was understandably offended. "What are you even talking about if not the kitchen paint?"

"Maggie." Harper was at the end of her rope. "We came here because we found her body here two nights ago. We were hoping if her ghost remained behind that it would be here. That might not be the case, though, because there's a very good chance that Maggie didn't die here."

"Oh." Realization slowly dawned on Zander. "Ghosts usually hang close to where they died, not necessarily where their body was discovered. You're very smart." He lightly tapped the end of Harper's nose. "That means we need to go to the Standish barn."

"That's exactly where we need to go."

Zander heaved out a sigh. "Fine. If it's gross in there, though, you're on your own."

"I'm well aware of your cleanliness rules."

"I mean it."

"I know you do." Harper also knew that Zander wouldn't abandon her in the barn with a ghost possibly close by and a murderer on the loose no matter how dirty it was. He simply liked to complain. "We should head out there now. If we expect to get answers, Maggie is the one person who can give them to us."

"So ... let's do it. On the way out there, we can stop by Home Depot since it's right on the way and get some paint samples."

"Ugh." Harper was beyond exasperated. "When are you going to let this go?"

"When your kitchen is pink."

"So ... never?"

"If that's how you want it to be."

"I've only been up two hours and I already need a nap."

"Try taking some vitamin D supplements. They'll make you feel better ... as will a pink kitchen."

"I can't even look at you right now."

## 7

# SEVEN

Harper made a face upon exiting Zander's vehicle in front of the Standish barn and catching sight of Mel's cruiser.

"I guess we weren't the only ones who thought it was a good idea to check this place out, huh?" Zander didn't bother to look at Harper, instead focusing his attention on the paint samples he held in his hand. "This is called Heartbreaker. What do you think of it?" Zander held up a color that made Harper involuntarily shudder.

"I think my heart would break having to look at that color for the rest of my life."

Zander offered an exaggerated expression that was both twisted and somehow cute. "The rest of your life? You only stick with a kitchen color for three years. Give me a break."

Harper abandoned her interest in the barn and focused on Zander. "Since when is that the rule?"

"It's always been the rule. Everyone knows you get bored of a color in three years."

"I've never heard that rule."

"You never heard the rule about not making a slurping noise when sharing my soda at the movie theater either and yet some things should just be common sense."

Harper rolled her eyes. "Whatever. I'm not painting my kitchen that color. It's never going to happen."

"Do you want to bet on it?"

"Sure." Harper turned back to the barn and pulled up short when Mel and Jared walked through the open door. They looked as surprised to see Harper and Zander as the ghost-hunting duo was to see them. "Hey."

"Hello, Heart." Jared recovered quickly. "Not that I'm not happy to see you or anything, but what are you doing here?"

"Looking for Maggie's ghost." Harper saw no reason to lie. "We went to the cemetery first, but we have no way of knowing if Maggie was killed there and since we know she was still alive – at least for a little bit – while here, this seemed like the place to start."

"Oh, well, smart." Jared was used to hearing about ghosts so he didn't even blink an eye at Harper's explanation. "Anything yet?"

"We just got here. The only thing we've had time to do is argue about paint colors."

"Ah." Jared shifted his eyes to Zander and frowned when he saw the paint strip Zander was staring at. "I will never agree to that color."

"There are four colors on here," Zander pointed out.

"And they're all so ugly I wish I was color blind."

"Ugh. You have no taste." Zander focused on Harper. "Don't listen to him. I think Heartbreaker is the way to go."

"I'm going to pass." Harper turned a pretty smile to Jared. "You're not going to give us grief about being here, are you? I was a little worried when I saw your cruiser, but then I figured you would probably be fine with it so ... you're fine with it, right?"

Jared was amused despite himself. "Would you stop if I wasn't?"

"No."

"Then I'm fine with it." Jared arched an eyebrow when he realized Zander and Mel were discussing paint colors, their heads tilted together as they stared at the brightly-colored strips. "We're not picking any of those colors."

"This one really isn't that bad," Mel argued, snagging the sample from Zander's hand and holding it up. "It's called Pink Cadillac. What's classier than that?"

"Whatever." Jared placed his hand at the small of Harper's back. "Come on. I'll go back through the barn with you. It's absolutely filthy. I want to make sure you don't accidentally trip and get hepatitis."

Harper beamed. "That's the best offer I've had all day."

## "UGH. WHAT A HOLE."

Zander was beside himself when he saw the state of the barn.

"That's pretty much what I said." Jared leaned against the wall as he watched Harper pick her way through the garbage. "Heart, be really careful. You could get something disgusting – and potentially incurable – if you touch the wrong thing."

"Believe it or not, I've seen worse than this," Harper noted. "I've even seen this place looking worse than this. Who ran the party this year, though? They're supposed to clean before leaving."

"That's a good question and I'm trying to find out the answer." Mel grabbed a garbage bag from the bar counter and opened it. "We could do a little something to clean things up before we leave, though, just to make sure there's no food around."

"I don't see why the food is such big deal." Zander wrinkled his nose. "It's the stale beer that smells."

"Yes, Milwaukee's Best." Harper was amused as she scented a cup. "Ah, it brings back fond memories of college parties."

"You must have been going to parties without me because I never attended a party where they served Milwaukee's Best," Zander complained.

"You did. You just didn't know it. In fact ... ." Harper broke off as a hint of movement caught her attention out of the corner of her eye. She tilted her head to the side and focused on a dark corner of the upstairs loft. "Huh."

Jared followed her gaze. "Do you see something?"

Harper nodded.

"A ghost?"

Another nod.

"Is it Maggie?" Mel was the one who asked the obvious question. "If she could point us to who hurt her, that would be great."

"I thought you didn't believe in ghosts," Jared sneered.

"I don't, but if Harper can point us in the right direction, I'm always happy to listen."

Harper shook her head as she stared at the dark figure. It was more of a shadow than a fully-formed ghost, although Harper had no doubt she could change that if she pushed hard enough. "It's not Maggie."

Jared stilled, surprised. "What do you mean? Are you saying there's another ghost up there? Should we be looking for another body?"

"I doubt it." Harper carefully made her way up the steps, doing her best to ignore the way the rickety wood swayed under her body weight. Jared followed – clearly unhappy – and allowed her to lead the way.

"Tell me what you see," Jared prodded, risking a glance over the railing to make sure Mel and Zander were still close and not finding trouble before focusing his full attention on his girlfriend. "Is it a young woman?"

Harper shook her head as she pursed her lips. "It's an old man."

The ghost picked that moment to float forward, his craggy ethereal skin glinting under the limited light as he murdered Harper with a dark glare. "I am not old! Do you have any idea how obnoxious it is to call someone old?"

Harper's lips curved. "I'm sorry. I didn't realize how rude I was being. What term do you prefer? Elderly?"

"That's even worse."

"Uh-huh. You tell me how you would like me to refer to your age and I'll be happy to do it."

The ghost made a face. "I'm in the prime of my life."

"You're dead so that doesn't really seem possible to me." Harper scanned the loft before meeting the ghost's steady gaze. "Who are you? I haven't seen you around before and yet you look as if you've been here a long time."

"And we're back to me being old."

Harper pressed her lips together and gathered her patience, ultimately opting for a different tack. "My name is Harper Harlow. I was born here in Whisper Cove. What about you?"

"Harlow?" The ghost made a face. "Are you any relation to Eunice Harlow?"

It took Harper a moment to track the name through her family tree. "Eunice was my great-grandmother. I never met her."

"Great-grandmother? Ugh. Maybe I am old."

Harper shrugged. "You look great for your age."

"How old do I look?"

"Does it matter? You knew my great-grandmother. That means you look great for your age."

"Good point." The ghost extended his hand as if he expected Harper to follow society's rules and shake it. "My name is Ezra Standish. What are you doing in my barn?"

"Oh, you're Mr. Standish." Harper exhaled heavily, relieved. "I guess it makes sense that you would be out here ... although I swear I've never seen you before."

Jared watched the exchange with overt curiosity but didn't insinuate himself into the conversation. He knew Harper would relate everything to him when she was done and her instincts, while not infallible, were almost always spot on.

"Why can you see me at all?" Ezra asked, genuinely curious. "I've been around people for years – decades, really – and you're the only one to ever notice me."

Harper felt inexplicably sad about the admission. "I'm sorry. If I knew you were here I would've come sooner to help you cross over. I guess I never thought to check."

Jared stirred. "Wait ... didn't you say you came to these parties when you were younger?"

"Twice, but we never stayed," Harper replied. "I don't do well with crowds ... especially when people know what I can do because they always ask a lot of questions. Questions make me uncomfortable."

"I can see that."

"I don't remember you coming to the parties, but I'm kind of glad that's the case," Ezra offered. "You have no idea how much I hate those parties ... I mean, like really hate them."

"I'm sure they're annoying from your perspective," Harper agreed. "Do you spend all your time in this barn?"

Ezra shrugged. "Where else? My house is long gone."

"And yet the barn remains," Harper mused. "I never really considered that. The barn is out here in what looks to be the middle of nowhere and there's no house. Where did the house used to be?"

Ezra pointed to the east. "That way, close to the trees. It's long gone, though. Even the stone wall that was along the back of the house has completely disappeared as far as I can tell. There's only a little line now ... and the storm cellar is still there but hidden. I know because some people were on the property using a measuring tape one day – I have no idea when because time means nothing to me – and one of them tripped over the door and found the storm cellar."

"Hmm." Harper stared through the filthy window but came up empty. "So, you spend all your time out here alone and once a year people show up and throw a party in the middle of your digs before taking off."

"It feels more regular than that. The parties, I mean. They usually don't leave things such a mess out here either."

"Yeah, this is disgraceful," Harper agreed. "I think Mel is going to make some calls and get people out here to clean the space. They should be ashamed for leaving it like this."

"And if it's not done by the end of the day, I'm going to have this barn completely closed off and that will be the end of the party," Mel added darkly.

"I would be all for that." Ezra flicked his eyes to Jared. "Who is your silent friend? How come he's not doing any talking?"

"He can't hear you." Harper opted for honesty. "I have a special ability."

"To talk to ghosts?"

"Yes."

"It seems to me that's not a very good ability. You must have ticked off somebody up high to be saddled with that."

Harper shrugged. "I used to believe that when I was a kid. I thought I was being punished for ... something, maybe because I was bad. I spent a lot of years trying to find out why it happened to me and still more years trying to ignore what I could do."

"And now?"

"And now I'm fine with what I can do and I believe it really is a gift," Harper replied, matter-of-fact. "I can help you, in fact. You're probably lucky to be so together given how long you've been on your own. Most ghosts who hang around long after their deaths go a little nutty."

"I guess I like being nutty rather than old."

"Who wouldn't?" Something occurred to Harper. "Give it a little time and decide if you want me to help you. If you don't, I understand, but I swear there's something better out there waiting for you. I mean ... you probably have a wife waiting for you on the other side. You must miss her."

"She was a real pill ... and not one I ever wanted to swallow." Ezra was grim. "I'll consider it. I'm mostly fine here, though, except for the parties."

"Speaking of the parties, do you hang around when they're going on?" Harper had an idea she wanted to explore. "Do you watch the kids and what they do?"

Ezra nodded. "I don't really have a choice in the matter. If someone doesn't watch them then things will get out of hand."

Harper furrowed her brow. "How do you stop things from getting out of control?"

"I shut off the lights and break windows."

Harper snickered. "That's why people think this place is haunted. Things move, stuff breaks. I always thought it was stories, but I really should've checked this place out before now. That's on me. I'm sorry."

"Don't apologize. It's fine. Other than the parties, I don't really pay attention to it all."

"Well, still, if you were here the night of the party, that means you might have seen something of interest," Harper suggested, holding out her hand to Jared. "Give your phone to me, please."

Jared did as asked without questioning Harper's motivations.

Harper sorted through the photos until she came up with what she was looking for and held up the screen. "This is Maggie Harris. She was here three nights ago. She turned up dead in the cemetery two nights ago. I don't suppose you saw her while she was here, did you?"

Ezra was serious as he leaned closer and stared at the screen. "Pretty girl."

"She was," Harper agreed. "To my knowledge, she was also a good girl. She didn't get in a lot of trouble or anything. She minded her own business. Something happened to her, though, and we're trying to find out what."

"I remember her." Ezra was calm, unruffled. "She came with another woman. They both had their faces painted like they were trying to catch every fly in the place in their ointment."

Harper wrinkled her forehead as she tried to untangle the words. Finally, she gave up. "I don't know what that means."

"It means that she had stuff all over her face and looked like a whore." Ezra clearly wasn't one to mince words. "Women in my day didn't paint their faces that way."

"Oh, well, right." Harper was understandably uncomfortable. "It was Halloween, though. I'm sure it was part of her costume." At least Harper was hopeful that was true. "As for Maggie, did you see her with anyone that night while she was here?"

Ezra shrugged. He looked as if he was losing interest in the conversation. "She talked to everyone. She drank a lot, danced a lot, and talked a lot. I didn't see her with any one person. She was with everyone. She even kissed a few people, too."

"A few people." Harper cocked an eyebrow. "Like kissed in a friendly way or in a romantic way?"

"Is there a difference?"

"Well, yeah. I kiss him in a romantic way and the one on the ground in a friendly way." Harper gestured between Jared and Zander. "They're definitely different."

"My kisses are better, right?" Jared winked.

"Obviously." Harper wiped her sweaty palms over the seat of her jeans. "I'm just trying to get a picture here, Ezra. You said Maggie was hanging all over and kissing everyone. Did she wander off with anyone?"

"I honestly don't know," Ezra answered. "I didn't pay attention to her over anyone else. In truth, I was more interested in the people making a mess. The only thing I can say about her is that she didn't make a mess."

"Well, at least she had that going for her," Harper muttered, flicking her eyes to Jared. "He doesn't know. He said she was here and hanging around with a bunch of people ... maybe kissing more than one of them."

"Definitely kissing more than one of them," Ezra stressed. "She was giggling like a maniac and smoking tiny little cigarettes. They didn't even have filters."

"Oh." Harper licked her lips. "Have you seen Maggie's autopsy yet?"

Jared shook his head. "No. Why?"

"Ezra says she was smoking pot. Maybe you should run a full toxicology report on her. I'm not saying the pot had anything to do with this, but maybe she was drugged or something."

"That's something to consider." Jared absently ran his knuckles up and down Harper's back. "Is that it? I was kind of hoping you would come up with a direction for us to look."

"I was kind of hoping for that, too," Harper admitted ruefully. "I guess that's not going to happen, at least today."

"Bummer."

"Totally."

## 🦂 8 🦂

## EIGHT

Jared and Mel left Harper and Zander at the barn and returned to the office to look over Maggie's autopsy results. There was nothing surprising in the report except for one little tidbit.

"Whoever killed her wiped down the body," Jared noted, cocking his head to the side. "She had residue around her neck, one like you might find on those wipe things you can buy at any grocery store."

"I noticed that, too." Mel leaned back in his chair as he sipped his coffee. "There's no way to track down where the wipes were purchased – especially since whoever used them could've had them stored for years, for all we know – so I think it's a dead end."

"It's still interesting." Jared chewed on his bottom lip. "What do you make about what Harper said?"

"I have no idea what you're talking about."

"The ghost. The Ezra Standish guy."

"I know you don't want to hear this, but I have trouble believing she was talking to a ghost," Mel said. "I don't happen to believe in Harper's abilities the same way you do."

"And yet you know she can do something." Jared wasn't in the mood to fight with his partner, but he felt the need to stand up for Harper all the same. "Why would she make up having a conversation with Ezra Standish of all people? Other than confirming Maggie was at the barn party – which we already knew – he didn't tell us anything of note."

"Which is exactly why I'm suspicious."

"Whatever." Jared sank into silence, only breaking it when he realized he was desperate to get the last word. "Do you want to know what I think?"

"Probably not, but I'm sure you're going to tell me." Mel remained focused on his computer screen. "Lay it on me."

Jared ignored his tone and barreled forward. "I think you do believe her, but you don't want to believe her because realizing that ghosts are real ... and out there ... means that we're pretty small in the grand scheme of things, kind of like ants on a picnic blanket. No one wants to feel small."

"Oh, that was almost profound." Mel made a condescending face. "Can we be done talking about your girlfriend and turn to the business at hand?"

Jared nodded. "Sure. I just want you to know that I'm here if you ever have any questions."

Mel heaved out a sigh. "You're not going to let this go, are you?"

"Nope." Jared shook his head. "If I can't answer your questions, I'm sure Harper will be more than willing to sit down with you."

"That's exactly what I'm afraid of," Mel grumbled, shaking his head. "Anyway, back to what's important; the medical examiner believes our killer is of normal height and stature. He says between five-foot-eight and five-foot-ten. I think the only thing we can garner from that is that the killer is a man."

"Or a really tall woman," Jared countered. "Harper is tall."

"She is, but she's not *that* tall and Whisper Cove isn't known for model-sized women," Mel pointed out. "The medical examiner also said that our killer has large hands – also signifying a man – and there was no hesitation."

"So that means we're either dealing with a sociopath who had no problem looking into an innocent woman's eyes as he snuffed the life out of her or someone who has done this before," Jared mused. "Which one are you leaning toward?"

"I don't know. I can't think of any reason for someone to want to kill Maggie."

"I can." Jared surprised himself with his response.

"You can?" Mel arched an eyebrow. "Would you mind sharing with the class?"

"She worked for a bank."

"So?"

"So she worked for a bank," Jared repeated. "She worked for a bank, which means someone might have thought she had access to money. Money is one of the biggest murder motivators out there."

"Huh." Mel stroked his chin. "I never really considered that until you said it out loud, but I guess it makes sense. Most people don't understand how a bank works. They naturally assume all tellers and workers have access to the vault, which is not the case."

"So maybe we're not really looking for a killer," Jared suggested. "I mean ... we're obviously looking for a killer. We might be looking for a thief, too, though."

"That's a good place to start." Mel wagged his finger. "Let's head to the bank."

"I thought you would never ask."


## "WHAT ARE YOU DOING?"

After filling his stomach with tomato soup and a grilled cheese sandwich, Zander was sleepy and ready for a nap. That's why Harper's intense face as she studied the menu on the wall at the diner made him leery.

"I'm looking at the menu."

"You just ate the world's best tomato soup."

"I did and it was good." Harper's eyes were lit with enthusiasm as she locked gazes with Zander. "Do you want to help me plan a special surprise for Jared?"

"Is that a trick question?"

"No. I'm serious." Harper dug into her purse for money. "We don't have a tour tonight because the cemetery is shut down due to finding Maggie's body. That's a rarity for a Monday during the Halloween season. I want to do something nice for Jared with my break."

"That's really what you were sitting there thinking about?" Zander was disgusted. "If you're going to waste brain power thinking of something other than work, why not focus on paint samples?" Zander grabbed his pink stack of torture and fanned it out. "How do you feel about Tutti Frutti?"

"I will kill you if you don't stop asking me about pink colors for a kitchen that is going to be blue," Harper gritted out. "I'm not kidding."

"I think I'm starting to wear you down."

"You're starting to make me look forward to moving away from you," Harper countered. "I doubt that's your intended purpose but ... there it is."

Zander heaved out a dramatic sigh. "Fine. I'll help you plan a romantic night for the best friend stealer."

Harper grinned. "Thank you."

"I'm still your favorite person in the world, right?"

"One of them."

"Oh, no." Zander refused to back down. "The number one spot has always been mine and it will always be mine. I want you to promise."

"What if I have a kid?" Harper challenged. "Do you expect to get the top spot over a child?"

"I haven't decided yet. It depends on if the kid is a pain in the butt or like me."

Harper narrowed her eyes. "That sounds like the same thing to me. Like you or a pain in the butt. I'm not really seeing a difference there."

"Ha, ha. That's not the way to get me to help you plan a romantic night with your color-blind boyfriend."

"Fine." Harper adopted her most rational tone. "You're still my favorite."

"Great. I'll help you romance Jared's socks off. What did you have in mind?"

"I'm glad you asked. How do you feel about a picnic?"

"No. It's October. Picnics are for the summer."

"I was thinking of an indoor picnic ... at the new house."

"Oh, well ... I've heard worse ideas." Zander shrugged. "Is it wrong that I hope he gets ants in his pants?"

"Yes."

"It doesn't feel wrong."

"Well, it is."

"You're absolutely no fun sometimes."

"I'm fine with that."


**MARK CROWLEY WAS THE** same age as Mel. They'd known each other since high school and had something of a tempestuous relationship. That was the first thing Jared picked up on as he sat in one of Crowley's guest chairs.

"Hello, Mel." Mark wore an expensive suit and combed his hair to cover a rather pronounced bald spot. "Long time no see."

"Yes, I believe our last conversation – and it was a lovely one – was when I came in for a loan two years ago and you told me no," Mel sneered.

Jared shifted on his seat, uncomfortable. "Um ... you guys know each other, huh?"

"Unfortunately," Mel muttered.

"I didn't turn you down for that loan because I was trying to be a jerk," Mark offered. "I turned you down because I didn't think you needed a mid-life crisis mobile."

Mel's mouth dropped open as Jared fought the mad urge to laugh. "That was a Camaro! It was not a mid-life crisis mobile."

"That's always what a Camaro is," Mark argued. "I didn't make up the rules, but I recognized what was going on and decided to save you. You should be thankful, not obnoxious."

"Can you believe this guy?" Mel looked to Jared for help.

"I have to agree on the Camaro," Jared said. "If any car screams 'mid-life crisis,' it's a Camaro. Well, that and a Mustang convertible."

"Oh, I cannot even talk to you." Mel held up his hand to silence his partner and sucked in a breath. "We're not here to rehash old problems, Mark. We are here to talk about a new one, though."

"Oh, well, I can't wait," Mark drawled, steepling his fingers on his lap as he leaned back in his chair. "What stupid thing do you want to buy now?"

"We're not here on personal business," Jared interjected. "We're here to talk about Maggie Harris."

Mark turned serious and his smile slipped. "Yeah. I heard about that. I honestly couldn't believe it when the news started filtering through the grapevine. She was always such a good worker ... I mean, a really good worker."

"What can you tell us about her?" Mel asked, clicking his ink pen as he pulled out a small notebook. "I honestly don't know much about her. She never got in a lot of trouble as a kid. That's good for her but that kind of leaves me out in the cold."

"I'm not sure what you're looking for," Mark hedged. "I heard that you were looking at Maggie's death as a possible murder, but I didn't really believe it until just now. I want to help, though, so tell me what kind of information you're looking for and I'll see if I can point you in the right direction."

"That sounds good," Jared said. "For starters, how was she as a worker?"

"About what you would expect. She was a teller, which means she did basic stuff. I wouldn't exactly call it a hard job, but she always showed up for her shift and didn't try to leave early unless she had an important appointment. She did use all of her sick days every year, though."

"Isn't that what they're for? To use, I mean."

"Yes, but most people bank a few in case they get seriously ill," Mark explained. "Maggie was the opposite. She used all her days and would try to get more whenever possible."

"I thought you said she was a good worker," Mel challenged.

"She was. She was also a big fan of partying. Both her and Heather liked to take three-day weekends quite often. Since this is a bank and we already get three-day weekends more than most people, I'm sure you can imagine how that went."

"I guess," Jared agreed. "So, Heather and Maggie were party

mongers by nature. Do you happen to know who they hung around with?"

"I think they had a regular crowd that met at that one bar over on Hall Road in Macomb County." Mark screwed up his face in concentration. "They met twice a week. It's that bar with all the games. Um ... Dave & Buster's, I think that's what it was called."

"I know the place you're talking about," Jared said. "I've been considering taking Harper and Zander there one day over the winter. I'm always looking for things to entertain Zander."

"I think their group isn't set as much as it's just a known thing that people meet at that bar," Mark said. "As far as who Maggie hung around with, I mostly saw her with Heather. She dated occasionally, but I don't think she stuck with one guy for more than a few weeks."

"Was that her choice?"

"That's a good question." Mark licked his lips. "Listen, I don't want to speak ill of the dead, but Maggie was the type who wanted very specific things from men. She wasn't a bad girl, but she was a bit ... um ... materialistic."

Jared and Mel exchanged a quick look.

"I don't know what that means," Jared said after a beat. "Can you be more specific?"

"She was always looking for someone with money," Mark replied. "She didn't care about age or looks, but she cared about money."

"Oh." Jared didn't know what to make of that. "So she didn't have a regular boyfriend, but she was looking for a specific type. Can you think of anything else?"

"I really can't."

"Just for clarification, did Maggie have access to the vault?" Mel asked.

Mark immediately started shaking his head. "Only the managers and floor leaders have access to the vault. They're intermediaries between the tellers and me. If you're thinking that someone killed Maggie for access to the vault, there's no way. She didn't have a key."

"Okay. Thanks. We'll be in touch."

**HARPER AND ZANDER MADE** a stop before heading home and it was to the one place Harper didn't want to see again until next Halloween. Unfortunately for her, she knew that wish wouldn't be answered because the cemetery would essentially be her second home for the next week.

"I just want to check to make sure that we can lead another tour tomorrow and they're not answering the office phone," Harper said as she climbed out of Zander's truck on the side road that led to the main cemetery building. "You can wait here for me. I shouldn't be more than five minutes."

"Fine. I don't want to talk to Douglas anyway."

Harper snickered. "He's not so bad. He's just a little ... peculiar. What do you expect from the guy who willingly runs the cemetery?"

"He's still weird." Zander changed the radio station and smiled when Celine Dion's voice took over. "Oh, I love this song even though it reminds me of *Titanic*."

"I thought you hated that movie."

"If she'd just moved over on that stupid piece of wood they both could've survived and you know it!"

Harper grinned. She loved winding up Zander. "I know. Just for the record, listening to Celine Dion is kind of stereotypical for a gay guy. You know that, right?"

"It's not stereotypical. She sings like a dream."

"Yeah, yeah." Harper shut the truck door and passed in front of the vehicle. To save time she planned to cut through the very thin woods so she could check the building herself. Instead, she caught the glint of metal through the trees and cut to her left.

Zander noticed she was going in the wrong direction and rolled down his window. "Where are you going?"

"There's a car or something over here." Harper furrowed her brow and didn't bother glancing over her shoulder. "I just want to see."

"There's no car," Zander scoffed, killing the engine of his truck and hopping out. "That's just an empty ... oh, that is a car." He made a face when he walked through the line of trees and frowned at the small Ford Escort. "Why would someone park a car here?"

"That's a very good question," Harper murmured as she moved to the window and peered inside.

Zander tried to open the door but it didn't work. "It's locked."

"Yeah, but what does that look like to you?" Harper pointed at a folder sitting in the middle of the passenger seat. "Isn't that a Whisper Cove Banking & Loan folder?"

Zander nodded. "What do you think that means?"

"That maybe this is Maggie's car. I mean ... I didn't ask Jared about it because it didn't really occur to me that it might be an issue, but if this is Maggie's car, maybe she drove herself here."

"Does that mean you're calling Uncle Mel and the boy wonder?"

Harper smiled as she fished for her phone. "I'm totally telling Jared you see him as Robin in his partnership with Mel."

"Good. I find it funny when his head twists around like that kid in *The Exorcist*. Tell him to hurry. Your food is going to have to be warmed as it is. You don't want Jared blowing his entire night on work when you have a special event planned for him, do you?"

Harper shook her head. "Good point. I'm on it."

#### NINE

Harper was a ball of nerves as she waited next to the car for Jared and Mel. They arrived ten minutes later, but she was dancing on the balls of her feet when Jared cut through the trees.

"I think this is Maggie's car."

Jared arched an eyebrow as he took in her excitable countenance. "Okay." He stared at her for a long beat and then shook his head. "Good find, tiger."

Harper realized he was teasing her and made a face. "I'm sorry. I just ... got worked up."

"It's okay." Jared lightly chuckled as he circled the car, using his hand to block out the sun as he pressed his face to the window and looked inside. "That looks like a folder from the bank."

"That's what I said."

"Well ... good." Jared flicked his eyes to a bored-looking Zander. "How come you're not as enthusiastic about finding the car as your partner in crime?"

"Because I have better things to do." Zander held up a paint sample sheet. "What do you think of this one? It's called 'Bright and Shiny People' and I think it has a warm glow."

Jared's smile faltered. "Absolutely not. "Are you trying to kill me?"

"I'm not going to rest until your kitchen is pink."

"Then you'd better find someone to turn you into a vampire because that's never going to happen," Jared shot back.

"Can you guys stop making all that racket?" Mel complained as he moved to the back of the vehicle and tapped the license plate information into his phone. "I don't see why you guys always have to make things so dramatic."

"We're on the same wavelength, Uncle Mel," Zander drawled as he flipped through the paint samples. "What do you think of 'Pleasant Day Pink'?"

Now it was Mel's turn to make a face. "I think no man wants his kitchen to be pink, kid," Mel replied dryly. "That's a chick color."

Zander's disdain was withering. "I'm a man and I happen to love pink. Are you suggesting I'm not a man because I happen to be gay?"

Mel balked. "You know that's not true. You're my favorite nephew."

Zander snorted. "I'm your only nephew."

"That doesn't mean I'm not genuinely fond of you." Mel meant it. "Pink is a girl color, though. It makes men think of ... soft things ... and a kitchen shouldn't be a place to think about soft things."

Harper cocked her head as she met Jared's gaze. "Does pink make you think of soft things?"

Jared shook his head. "No. You make me think of soft things. When I look at you, though, I see blue."

"Really?" Harper was intrigued. "When I look at you I see gray, but not a weak gray. It's more of a strong charcoal gray. I wonder why that is."

"I know why I see the blue," Jared supplied. "It's because of your eyes. I always associate you with blue because of what I see when I look into your eyes, and now that is my favorite color."

Harper beamed. "You're so sweet."

Jared returned the smile. "I do my best."

"Just out of curiosity, what was your favorite color before it changed to blue?"

"Ironically, it was gray."

Harper's smile grew. "I think we're a good match."

Jared lightly tapped her forehead as he gave her a quick kiss, ignoring the way Mel groaned and the annoyed face Zander made. "I think we are, too. What do you have on the license plate, Mel?"

"It's Maggie's car," Mel replied, moving to the driver's side of the vehicle and looking inside. "It's locked. We could break the window, but I think it would be smarter to have the state police tech team take it and go through it."

"I think that's our best bet, too." Jared idly ran his hand up and down Harper's back. He tried to be professional at work but sometimes forgot. "I'm kind of curious how it ended up out here. Do you think that means Maggie drove herself to the cemetery?"

Harper was intrigued by the prospect. "I don't know. Why would she do that? Plus, I got the feeling that she was drinking pretty heavily at the party. She probably shouldn't have been driving at all."

"We talked to Mark Crowley at the bank," Mel volunteered. "He said Maggie was a decent worker but interested in partying as much as possible."

"That's not all he said," Jared reminded him. "He also said that Maggie was on the lookout for a rich man to get in good with. Apparently she didn't care about looks or personality. Money was key to her."

"Huh." Harper rubbed her hands together, uncomfortable. "I didn't know Maggie very well even though I was only a few years older than her. She always struck me as shallow. I was feeling bad about thinking those things about her when I realized she was dead ... but now I'm starting to wonder if she was even more shallow than I realized."

"I think that shallow is probably a good word." Jared stared into the car a second time. "It doesn't look as if there's much in there, but we might luck out. For all we know there's something in the trunk."

"Just out of curiosity, why would Maggie drive herself to the cemetery on a Friday night after the barn party?" Zander queried. "I mean ... if her whole thing was hooking up, why would she come here alone?"

"We don't know that she came here alone," Mel argued. "She could've had someone with her."

"She might not have even driven her own car," Jared added. "For all we know something happened at the barn and whoever killed her panicked and drove her here."

"You make it sound like an accident," Harper countered. "I don't think what happened to Maggie can be misconstrued as an accident."

"Oh, don't misunderstand, I don't think it was an accident," Jared clarified. "We got the autopsy results. There was no hesitation when it came to doing the deed. That doesn't mean someone didn't panic after killing her, though. We simply don't know what we're dealing with."

"I guess." Harper rubbed the back of her neck. "Do you need anything else from us?"

"No." Jared shook his head. "I shouldn't be too far behind you. Go home. Get comfortable. I'll be there as soon as I can."

"That's the plan." Harper gave him a quick kiss. "When you do get off, come to the new house, okay? I'll be waiting for you there."

Jared furrowed his brow. "You will? How come?"

Harper's face split with a genuine smile. "It's a surprise."

"Really?" Jared's curiosity was officially piqued. "Then I will be there as soon as I can."

"I'm looking forward to it."

"I am, too," Zander said, turning a paint sample sideways. "I'm now leaning toward Salmon Surprise."

"Ugh." Jared made a face. "I'm not painting my kitchen Salmon Surprise."

"You're absolutely no fun."

"Yeah, yeah."

**JARED WAS ABOUT SEVENTY** minutes behind Harper and when he let himself into the new house, he couldn't help being surprised given the number of candles she'd lit and placed around the living room.

He grinned when he saw the air mattress she'd inflated – and proceeded to make up like a bed – and he didn't spy the picnic basket on the floor behind the couch until he was already stripping out of his coat.

"This looks nice."

Harper poked her head into the room and smiled. "You're here. I'm glad. I was starting to get a little worried."

"I was as quick as I could be." Jared draped his coat over the back of the couch and pursed his lips as he studied the room. "Not that I'm not impressed by what you've done here – and I really am, so don't get the wrong idea – but what's the occasion?"

Harper, holding a large cooking spoon in her hand, shrugged. "I thought we could use a night alone."

"Are you worried that I'm about to snap and kill Zander?"

Harper shook her head. "I'm worried that *I'm* about to snap and kill Zander."

Jared chuckled as he shuffled closer and gave her a quick kiss. "You're a strong woman to put up with him day in and day out."

"I love him."

"I know."

"He's a pain in the butt, though." Harper shook her head to dislodge the dark thoughts threatening to derail the evening. "Sit down on the blanket. Dinner is almost ready."

Jared studied the spoon with interest. "You cooked? How did you have time for that?"

"I picked up sandwiches and soup from the diner and heated it up. That's not cooking."

"You make it look good regardless." Jared smacked a loud kiss against her cheek and moved to the picnic blanket to sit, his eyes falling on the air mattress. "So ... are you trying to seduce me or something? If so, you shouldn't worry about putting too much effort into it because I'm pretty much a sure thing."

Harper chuckled from the kitchen, her back to Jared as she worked. "I thought we could use a night alone. I brought some catalogs and my laptop."

"That sounds ... fun." Jared wrinkled his nose. "Are you saying you don't want to seduce me? I was so looking forward to that."

"I'm going to seduce you. I just thought between rounds of seduction we could talk about house stuff while we're actually in the house and don't have Zander breathing down our necks."

"Ah." Jared brightened considerably. "You're saying we're going to spend the night here and enjoy nothing but each other for the next twelve hours or so."

"Basically."

"Sold." Jared yanked off his shoes and tossed them away from the blanket, looking up when Harper carried in two cute soup bowls on a tray. "That smells good."

"I wish I could say I made it, but I'm a terrible cook," Harper admitted, carefully lowering herself to the ground. "It does smell good, though."

"It definitely does." Jared dug in the picnic basket and came up with sandwiches. "This was a good idea."

"I thought so." Harper unwrapped her sandwich. "Zander helped me collect everything – including the candles – so I owe him a little bit. I'm still not painting our kitchen pink."

"No, pink is out of the question. Just blame it on me."

"I should be an adult and take it on myself."

"Or you could just blame it on me."

Harper grinned as she dipped the corner of her sandwich into her cream of broccoli soup. "Maybe I'll just blame it on you."

Jared returned the smile. "Good idea." He stretched out on his side and glanced around the living room. "I know you're concerned about furniture, but we could always use what Henry Spencer left behind when he died. His daughter didn't want it so it's technically ours to do with as we please. That will allow us some breathing room."

Harper shifted, uncomfortable. "I know this is going to sound weird given what I do for a living, but I don't want to sit on a dead guy's furniture."

Jared barked out a laugh. "Fair enough." He broke the corner off his sandwich and popped it into his mouth. "Can I ask you something?"

Harper bobbed her head. "Of course."

"Are you excited to live here with me?"

Harper widened her eyes. "Do you think I'm not excited?"

"I think you seem excited and a little nervous," Jared clarified. "It's a big deal."

"Living together?" Harper smirked. "I've been living with a guy for years. It's not such a big deal."

"Ha, ha." Jared poked her side. "You've been living with your best friend. Now you're moving in with the guy you love. That's different."

"That *is* different," Harper agreed. "I am really excited about it. I'm also a little nervous, which I was hoping you wouldn't pick up on. You're too perceptive."

"Do you want to know something? I'm a little nervous, too."

Harper brightened, hopeful. "You are? What are you nervous about?"

"Well, for starters, I have to wonder what's going to happen if you get bored and need someone to entertain you. I keep picturing having to walk over to the other house so I can collect you because Zander is the one you go to when you want to have fun. Of course, when I picture that, I see you and Zander clinging together as I try to wrench you free from his grip. I would appreciate it if that didn't happen."

Harper snorted. "That's not going to happen. I'm sure Zander and I will hang out, but I'm not a kid. I don't need constant entertainment. You don't have to worry about that."

"I'm also worried that you're going to miss Zander more than you like living with me." Jared felt exposed and lowered his eyes. "I'm legitimately fearful you'll spend two nights over here and change your mind."

Harper balked. "I would never do that."

"Because you don't want to upset me or because you wouldn't want to?"

"Because I wouldn't want to." Harper was firm. For some reason, Jared admitting his worries calmed her. "I worry about the same thing, though, for the record. I worry that we're going to get over here and you're suddenly going to come to your senses and realize I'm not very interesting without Zander constantly talking in my ear. What if you get bored?"

"Oh, I'll never get bored, Heart." Jared tipped up her chin with his thumb. "You're interesting all on your own. Truth be told, Zander makes you too interesting. I like you when we have one-on-one time."

Harper leaned so her forehead was resting against Jared's and sighed. "We're going to make this work, aren't we?"

Jared nodded without hesitation. "It's going to be an adjustment, but we're definitely going to make it work."

"We still have to get rid of this furniture."

"I'll see if I can put up a listing and unload it. I'll get it out of here as soon as possible."

"Good."

"Yeah." Jared gave her a quick kiss and then turned back to his sandwich and soup. "Let's eat and then get comfortable with our catalogs. I'm looking forward to making some decisions."

Harper's lips curved. "That makes two of us."

**FIVE HOURS LATER, ALL** the candles except one on the coffee table had been extinguished. Jared decided to leave that one to serve as a nightlight so no one would accidentally careen into a wall in the darkness.

The couple did exactly what they said they would. They played and then settled down to look at catalogs and talk about their future. Then they shifted from one sort of dreaming to another. It was there Harper found herself trapped now.

"Who is out there?"

She was fearful as she glanced around the dreamscape, her hand pressed close to her mouth as she scanned the darkness. Her heart pounded and she could swear she felt someone watching her. She wasn't one to believe in prophetic dreams but that didn't stop her from feeling afraid.

"I know you're out there," Harper rasped as she stared at trees she didn't recognize. "Show yourself. If you have something to say, say it."

No one answered. No one stepped forward. And still, Harper could hear movement in the distance. Even though she knew it was fruitless – dream logic never makes sense, after all – she started to run. Terror drove her to make the move and she couldn't stop herself.

She fought hard to stay upright as she zipped between the trees, hoping her natural athletic ability would allow her to remain fleet-footed as she attempted to outrun her pursuer.

The more she ran, the more terrified she got. She could feel something getting close, someone's fingers moving near enough to brush against her hair without grabbing it. With each step, her heart rate increased. With each smack of a branch against her face, her anxiety mounted until she burst free from the trees and ran smack dab into a faceless shadow.

Harper screamed when she felt a set of arms moving around her, and bolted to a sitting position on the air mattress in the middle of the living room in her new house. She sucked in a weighted breath and risked a glance to her right, where she found Jared calmly slumbering.

*Just a dream. It was just a dream.*

As if feeling a set of eyes watching her, Harper slowly shifted her gaze until it landed on something dark and filmy in the corner of the room. She recognized the ghost right away because she'd been looking for that female face for almost forty-eight hours.

"Maggie."

The ghost didn't say anything, instead shaking her head as she slowly disappeared. She was gone within seconds.

"What's wrong, Heart?" Jared murmured as he ran his fingers up and down her arm. "Do you feel okay?"

Harper forced herself to recline and rest her head on Jared's shoulder. "I'm fine. I had a dream. That will teach me to eat so much right before bed."

"It's okay." Jared's eyes remained closed as he petted the back of her head. "Go back to sleep. Think about what the new house will look like when we're done. That will lead to nice dreams."

Harper nodded as she shut her eyes. "That will be the best of all dreams."

She wanted to drift off right away, continue enjoying her night without a horrific pall hanging over her. It took more than an hour, though, and even then she was unsettled.

## ❧ 10 ☙

## TEN

Harper woke to find herself wrapped tightly around Jared, as if she were trying to bind herself to him, her face pressed securely against his chest. When she shifted her chin, she found him watching her with a baffled look.

"What's going on?" She instinctively wiped her mouth in case she'd drooled. "Was I snoring?"

"I thought you told me that you don't snore." Jared shifted so he could cradle her head while looking her up and down. "Has anyone ever told you that you resemble an angel when you sleep?"

Harper's cheeks flushed hot. "Um ... no. I think the snoring and drooling makes that impossible to believe."

"I happen to like both." Jared pressed a kiss to her forehead. "How did you sleep?"

"Um ... good."

Jared cocked an eyebrow. "That was a little too flippant for my taste. Didn't you sleep well?"

"I slept fine." *Except for the ghost I swear I saw staring at me from the corner of our new living room,* Harper silently added. "It's just weird waking up on the floor. You know I'm a slow starter. It takes me a while to figure out what's going on."

Jared wasn't convinced. "Heart, we're moving in together. If something is bothering you, I want to know what it is."

Harper balked. "It's not that something is bothering me."

"Then what is it?"

"Well ... I had a dream."

Jared didn't so much as blink. "Tell me about it." He knew she was prone to dark dreams at times. He figured it had something to do with her ability. The key was to remain calm when talking about it because it wasn't as if he could travel into her dreams and cheerfully murder what haunted her in an effort to save her peace of mind. "I can't help unless I know what happened in the dream."

Harper wasn't convinced he could help regardless, but she barreled forward anyway. "I was in the woods. I didn't recognize where ... it actually could've been anywhere or nowhere. Something was chasing me."

"Was it a person?"

"I think so."

"Could you see a face?"

Harper bit her bottom lip and shook her head. "No. It was more that I could feel someone chasing me. Then I managed to get to the edge of the trees and ran through ... and smacked into whatever was chasing me ... and I'm pretty sure it was a man without a face. Then I woke up."

"That must have been frightening." Jared traced soothing circles on the back of her neck. "It could've just been a standard nightmare because your subconscious is trying to work out what happened to Maggie."

"Yeah, well, the thing is ... um ... I think I saw Maggie's ghost watching me from the corner when I woke up."

Jared wrinkled his forehead, surprised. "You didn't mention that when you woke up last night." He glanced at the corner in question. "Do you see her now?"

Harper shook her head. "I'm not even sure I really saw her last night. It was as if she was there and then gone."

"Maybe she's still coming to grips with what happened to her." Jared was the pragmatic sort. He knew Harper didn't often overreact or see things that weren't there. Still, she was jerked from sleep. It was entirely possible she only thought she saw the dead woman's spirit. It was also possible Maggie followed Harper for some reason, and he was curious what that reason could be. "Do you think Maggie knew your secret? I mean, before she died, did she know you could see and talk to ghosts?"

"Do you mean in real life?" Harper shrugged as Jared massaged her shoulders. "That feels good."

Jared grinned. "Good. I'm actually surprised this air mattress was so comfortable to sleep on. We should consider spending more than the occasional night here while we get the house put together. We can think of it as fun little test runs."

"There's an idea." Harper was serious as she considered Jared's previous question regarding Maggie. "Maggie would've been a sophomore when Zander and I were seniors. I'm sure she at least heard some gossip about me. Everyone in town has heard at least a little something."

"You weren't close, though, right?"

Harper shook her head. "I was only close with Zander in high school. I was kind of afraid of everyone else. Okay, that's a slight exaggeration. I wasn't afraid of everyone else. It was more that I didn't want to hang around them because I was convinced they thought I was weird."

"It must have been difficult for you to be different in high school," Jared noted. "At that age, most kids simply want to be part of the popular crowd. Because of what you could do, people were probably afraid of you. I'm not saying it's right, but I can see it happening."

"It's not just that," Harper countered. "Word spread when I was really young, before I learned to keep my mouth shut about what I could see and hear. When we were in elementary school, parents told the kids to stay away from me because they thought I was disturbed."

While Jared enjoyed hearing stories about Harper and Zander's misspent youth, there was one exception. That exception revolved around anyone making fun of Harper. He'd seen photographs of her from that time and she was a small child, an angelic looking one with sad eyes and a lopsided smile, in fact. The idea of parents rallying their kids to bully her bothered him. "You weren't disturbed. You could see things the other kids couldn't. That doesn't make you disturbed."

Harper's smile was rueful. "Sometimes I think you get more worked up about defending my honor than I do."

"Well ... you weren't disturbed."

"Think about it from their point of view," Harper challenged. "What would you think if an eight-year-old said a ghost told her to do something?"

"I would believe her."

Harper snorted. "You would not. You would think she was disturbed, too."

"Not if it was you." Jared refused to back down. "I would always believe you no matter what."

"That's sweet, but we both know it's not true. You didn't believe me when we first met. It took a while for the trust between us to build. I'm not upset about the other parents not believing me. They were doing what they thought was best for their kids."

"Well, it was stupid." Jared made a face. "Their stupid kids would've been lucky to spend time with you and Zander."

"Funnily enough, that's what Zander believed, too. That's not exactly how it worked out, but I'm not sorry that Zander and I were forced into our own little group. I think it made me stronger over the long run."

Jared rolled so Harper was completely on top of him and he could stare into her eyes. "You're the strongest person I know. I'm not sure what that has to do with Maggie, though. You're basically saying she knew you could see and talk to ghosts, right?"

Harper nodded. "I'm saying she would've at least heard the rumors. I still don't understand why she ended up here instead of at the other house, though. Why would she come here looking for me?"

"Maybe she didn't. Maybe she followed you from the cemetery."

Harper arched an eyebrow, considering. "I didn't think about that. She could've been there the entire time, watching from the shadows. Maybe she did follow me home and only got up the courage to show herself when she thought I was the only one awake. Then, when she realized I was confused from the nightmare, she took off again."

"Or maybe she showed you the nightmare," Jared mused. "I mean ... maybe that wasn't a nightmare. Maybe that's essentially what happened to her."

Harper was dumbfounded. "How could she show me that?"

Jared shrugged. "I don't know. I wouldn't rule it out, though."

"I guess." Harper was conflicted. "I didn't see who was chasing her, though. I didn't see a face."

"Maybe that's because Maggie didn't see a face ... or at least didn't recognize the face she did see."

Harper tapped her bottom lip. "I didn't even consider that."

"Well, now you have something to think about." Jared gave her a solid kiss. "Now, here's something else to think about. I'm starving and we both need showers. I think that means we need to head back to the other house."

Harper absently nodded. "Yeah. I'm hungry, too."

"Let's pack up and get moving. We can talk about this more over breakfast."

"That sounds like a plan."


**"THAT SOUNDS LIKE** a really creepy dream," Shawn intoned sympathetically as he poured Harper and Jared mugs of coffee as they settled at the dining room table forty minutes later. "I'm sorry your romantic night was ruined because of that."

Jared exchanged an amused look with Harper as he dumped some Equal into his coffee. "Oh, our night wasn't ruined."

"Our night was fabulous," Harper agreed, her skin flushed from a long shower. "It was just the one part that was weird. Now that Jared has brought it up, though, I can't help but think he might be right. Maybe Maggie was trying to show me something."

"Maybe we should spend the afternoon trying to track down Maggie," Zander suggested as he flipped pancakes at the stove. He'd been unusually quiet since Jared and Harper returned to the house after their sexy sleepover across the way. "If she has something to say, it would be easier to understand through words than images."

86

"We'll be back at the cemetery tonight no matter what," Harper reminded him. "Did you get everyone rescheduled for tonight's tour?"

Zander nodded. "It's twice as big as our normal run."

"That can't really be helped. We only have so much time before Halloween. I don't want anyone to be disappointed."

Zander didn't bother to hide his eye roll. "You want the money for new furniture. Admit it."

"Fine. I want new furniture." Harper was sheepish. "I always put on a good show, though."

"You do," Zander agreed. "I called Molly and Eric to make sure they're around for the tour tonight. We might need extra voices of authority if people get out of hand."

In addition to being GHI's final two employees, Molly Parker and Eric Tyler were also Whisper Cove's newest couple. Even though Molly tried to hide her crush on Eric for what felt like forever, they finally hooked up ... and now were virtually inseparable.

"I'll be there, too," Jared said as he grabbed an orange from the bowl at the center of the table and began peeling it. "I want to see this tour in action and I think tonight is as good a night as any."

While the sentiment was sweet, Harper couldn't help being suspicious. She cast Jared a sidelong look as she tried to ascertain the level of his sincerity. "You didn't mention wanting to attend a tour before we stumbled across Maggie's body."

"That is not true." Jared split the orange in half and gave one helping to Harper. "Eat that. Vitamin C is good for you."

Harper peeled off a slice and made a big show of shoving it in her mouth, which made Jared smirk.

"As for wanting to tag along on a tour, I told you weeks ago that I wanted to see what you guys did on these tours," Jared said. "You said I could come whenever I found the time. I've found the time."

Harper remained unconvinced. "You're worried about me."

"Heart, I've been worried about you since we met." Jared's grin was too charming for Harper to remain angry. "If you expect me not to worry even more than usual given the fact that Maggie's body was found along your tour route – and her car was parked in the nearby bushes – then you're doomed for disappointment. I want to be there to make sure you're safe. I also want to see your performance. I don't think I'm being unreasonable."

"I don't think he's being unreasonable either," Shawn added. "I want to be there, too."

"Oh, it's going to be a full house," Zander drawled. "How fun does that sound? You're going to be like an ant under a magnifying glass, Harp. That won't cause you to freeze up or anything, will it?"

Harper frowned. "I'll be fine. I don't have performance anxiety ... like someone else I know."

Zander narrowed his eyes. "That happened one time. We were fourteen and you told me that ghosts were watching while I changed in the locker room. I was still traumatized at the thought when ... well, you know what ... happened."

Jared and Shawn exchanged amused looks. This was exactly the sort of childhood story they both enjoyed hearing.

"What did you think the ghost in the locker room was going to see?" Jared asked.

"That doesn't matter." Zander was prim as he focused on his pancakes. "Let's talk about something else."

"Yeah, we should definitely talk about something else," Harper agreed, winking at Jared before finishing her orange. "Tell me what you found out from the autopsy report. We didn't get a chance to talk about that much before we got distracted by catalogs and paint color dreams."

"Oh, now you're just messing with me," Zander grumbled. "You want me to ask about the paint colors and furniture, but I'm not going to do it."

"Stay strong, honey," Shawn encouraged. "I have faith you can do it."

"Yeah, yeah."

Jared kept his focus on Harper even though he was dying to poke Zander until he cracked like a holiday piñata. "Why do you want to know about the autopsy results?"

"Because I want to have all the details handy if I do manage to track down Maggie," Harper replied easily. "I know you said there was no hesitation when it came to the strangulation, but I'm curious if that means the killer is a professional or if it means something else I don't fully understand."

Jared considered arguing with her, forcing her out of the investigation for her safety. He knew that wouldn't work, though. Harper was headstrong and once she decided to investigate something, there was no turning her away. She would do it with or without him. Ultimately, he would rather she have all the information than to risk finding trouble because she was missing a piece.

"It could mean a few things," Jared hedged. "It could mean that Maggie was the initial target and the killer approached her knowing what he was going to do and he carried out his mission with minimal fuss."

"How can you be sure it's a man?" Shawn asked.

"The hand size was too big to belong to a woman unless she was a freak of nature," Jared replied, lifting Harper's hand for emphasis. "See Harper's hands here? Her hands are actually slightly big for a woman, but her fingers are still slender and her grip isn't strong. Whoever killed Maggie had a very strong grip and fingers twice as wide as what Harper has."

Harper stared at her fingers for a long beat. "Do you really think I have big hands for a woman?"

Jared snickered but ignored the question. "Another possibility is that Maggie was simply a victim of circumstance. Maybe she was in the wrong place at the wrong time. We still don't know how she got from the barn to the cemetery, and that will be the main thing we work on today.

"There's still another possibility, too," he continued. "There's a chance that Maggie was targeted by accident because the killer thought she was someone else – or maybe the killer thought she could offer something she couldn't – and once he committed to a path he had no choice but to follow through because he knew Maggie would open her mouth and end things for him otherwise."

"You're talking about the bank, right?" Harper queried. "You think someone could have targeted her because he thought she had access to a lot of money."

"She didn't," Jared said hurriedly. "We asked very specific questions.

The money she could've gotten her hands on wasn't exactly miniscule, but it wasn't all that large either. She didn't have a key to the vault, though. There was no way she could've gotten anyone access to the money stored in there. So either the killer was too stupid to know that or something else is going on.

"The truth is, we don't have a motive," he continued. "Maggie wasn't sexually assaulted, so that is seemingly off the table. Although we have no way of knowing if it was originally on the table and she fought back or if it was never a consideration. We basically have a lot of questions and no answers."

"What about DNA?" Shawn was fascinated by police work and had no inclination to hide his curiosity. "Did the medical examiner find anyone else's DNA?"

Jared nodded, causing Harper to widen her eyes.

"You didn't tell me that," Harper complained. "You guys might be able to track down a DNA match."

"We might, but we have no idea if the DNA is from Maggie's killer or some random person at the party," Jared pointed out.

"Oh." Harper deflated a bit. "I didn't even think of that."

Jared squeezed her hand as a form of solace. "Like I said, we have no idea what's going on or why it happened. Until we start getting answers instead of questions, we're in the dark."

"And that's really why you're coming to the tour tonight, right?"

Jared shook his head. "I'm coming because I want to see my girl in action."

"And?"

"And I want to make sure my girl is safe," Jared conceded. "I'm not going to feel guilty about that, so don't even try forcing my hand."

"Fine." Harper let loose a long-suffering sigh. "I guess I'll have to put up with being loved."

Jared's grin was sly. "And don't you forget it."

## ELEVEN

ELEVEN

Harper and Zander conducted an initial sweep of the cemetery and came up empty, Zander serving as watchdog as Harper called out to the elusive ghost. She never appeared.

With nothing better to do with the rest of their afternoon, the duo decided to head to the annual Whisper Cove Halloween Children's Extravaganza – which was held downtown and one of their favorite kid-friendly events – and waste several hours entertaining the younger set.

"You can really see ghosts, right?" Mikey Kaiser's eyes were so wide they looked as if they were going to pop out of his head. He was eight going on thirty and he always had a million questions whenever he crossed paths with Harper.

Harper nodded as she handed the boy, who happened to be dressed like some Pokémon thing Harper didn't fully recognize, a caramel apple. "I can really see ghosts."

"What do they look like? I mean ... are they covered in blood and guts and stuff?"

Harper risked a glance at Mikey's mother, Lacey Kaiser, and found her watching the scene with amusement rather than recrimination. "No. No blood and guts. They look like they did in life." That was mostly true, although Harper occasionally did run across ghosts who took the horrors of death with them to the other side. "Ghosts aren't something you need to be afraid of."

"I told him that already, but he won't listen," Lacey offered as she looked over the platter of caramel apples before selecting one. "He won't listen to me. I think it's a boy thing. His sister is two years older and never asks questions like that."

Harper flicked her eyes to Kasey Kaiser, a ten-year-old ball of energy dressed like a Bratz doll. The girl was holding court with a gaggle of similarly-dressed girls and laughing up a storm. "I think boys are naturally drawn to blood and guts. Except Zander, of course. I was more into getting dirty as a kid than him. For the most part, though, boys like that sort of thing."

"Oh, I definitely know that." Lacey took the open chair next to Harper and fixed Mikey with a pointed look. "Do you have anything else you want to ask Harper?"

Mikey, his mouth covered with caramel and sprinkles, nodded. "What?"

Mikey didn't immediately respond, which seemed to be the reaction his mother was expecting.

"How about you eat your apple and think about the questions over there with your friends?" Lacey suggested, pointing. "I want to talk to Harper for a few minutes and we can't do it with you around."

Mikey's gap-toothed smile slipped. "You want to talk about grown-up stuff, don't you?"

"Yes."

"I hate grown-up stuff."

"Then you won't want to be close for this conversation," Lacey said pragmatically. "Don't run with that apple – and especially the stick – stuck to your face like that. You'll choke if you trip."

"That might be cool." Mikey waved before taking off to join his friends near the hay bale maze.

"I bet he's fun," Harper said after a beat. "He seems pretty easygoing."

"He's not bad," Lacey agreed, leaning back in her chair. "I expect he'll be my favorite for the next couple of years. Kasey is already discovering boys and soon she'll be getting to that obnoxious age where she knows everything and won't shut up."

Harper had to admire Lacey's matter-of-fact nature. The woman was four years older than Harper but seemed a decade wiser. She wasn't the sort of mother who didn't see her children's faults. Instead, she accepted them and almost seemed amused at times when her kids did something other mothers would find embarrassing.

That was only one of the reasons Harper liked Lacey so much.

"I hope you're not upset because I told Mikey that ghosts were real," Harper hedged. "I know a lot of people get angry when I say that in front of their kids, but I happen to actually like you so I will feel bad if you're upset."

Lacey snorted. "Don't worry about it. I happen to believe ghosts are real and I can't see them."

Harper couldn't hide her surprise. "You do?"

Lacey nodded. "I've always believed. That was true even before you were a teenager and found that missing kid. You know the one who was in the car accident with her dead mother, right? You found her and I heard you explaining that the ghost mother led you to her.

"People were giving you a lot of grief back then because they thought you were making up the story and I remember feeling sorry for you," she continued. "I could tell you believed what you were saying. More importantly, there was no way for you to know where that car was – I mean, you couldn't see it from the road and you're the only reason rescue crews found it at all – so I never understood why people would rather believe you were making it up than getting help from the other side."

"Some people don't want to believe in ghosts because it's too much to rationalize," Harper explained. "I get it. It leads to questions, like why doesn't everyone come back as a ghost? How come everyone can't see ghosts? Are all ghosts good? Are some bad? Who decides who is a good and bad ghost?"

"All good questions," Lacey mused. "Have you come to any conclusions?"

Harper nodded without hesitation. "Souls don't change. If you're a good person in life, you'll most likely be a good ghost in death. There are a few random instances where that's not true, but more often than not it's because death was so traumatizing for the soul they simply can't rationalize what happened to them."

"That makes a lot of sense." Lacey finished her apple and dumped the stick and soiled napkins in a nearby trash receptacle. "I have a question for you and I'm kind of nervous to ask it. I don't see where I have any options, though, so I'm just going to come out with it."

Lacey's even nature caught Harper off guard. "Okay. Shoot."

"Is Maggie Harris running around as a ghost?"

Whatever question she was expecting, that wasn't it. Harper's mouth dropped open in surprise. "Why would you ask that?"

"Because she's the most recent person in Whisper Cove to die and everyone is talking about what happened to her," Lacey answered simply. "She was also flirting with my husband when she thought I wasn't looking and I'm understandably curious about what happened to her."

Harper swallowed hard as she ran the new information through her head. "I forgot that Craig works at the bank. He's a loan officer, right?"

Lacey bobbed her head and offered a friendly smile. "He is and he makes good money ... at least by Whisper Cove standards. Maggie spent the last year flirting with him and I'm ashamed to say that my initial reaction to hearing about her death wasn't exactly happiness, but it wasn't exactly sadness either."

"Oh, well ... ." Harper had no idea what to make of the situation. "I guess I can see that." She didn't know what else to say.

"Oh, your poor face." Lacey made a tsking sound as she shook her head. "Just for the record, I didn't kill her. My husband didn't either. We were at the Halloween party at the Elks lodge the night of the barn party and it's my understanding that's when Maggie was killed. We were on the decorating committee and there the whole night. You can check."

"I didn't think you killed her," Harper sputtered, finding her voice. "It's just ... I never pictured Maggie going after Craig. He's clearly a family man. You guys are still obviously in love after being married for eleven years. I saw you at the ice cream social this summer and you were sharing the same cone and holding hands. I remember thinking it was cute."

"We *are* still in love," Lacey confirmed. "Things aren't always perfect, but we make them work. That's why Craig told me when Maggie started flirting with him. He wanted me to be aware that he wasn't encouraging her in any way."

Now that she had a moment to consider what Lacey was saying, it made sense to Harper. "Mark Crowley said that Maggie was all about snagging a rich guy. While Craig isn't exactly rich, he would probably seem that way to Maggie if she was looking for someone with money to settle down with."

"Yeah, I don't think she really liked Craig as much as she liked the idea of what he could buy her," Lacey offered. "Still, I feel a little guilty about my initial reaction to the news of Maggie's death. No one deserves to die the way she did. I keep thinking that if she'd been allowed a few more years to mature that she probably would've grown out of this thing she had where money was the most important thing ... at least I hope that's true."

"I guess we'll never know." Harper absently scratched at the side of her nose. "As for Maggie's ghost, I don't know. I thought I saw her last night, but I can't be sure. It could've been a dream. Zander and I went looking for her this morning but came up empty."

"What does that mean?"

Harper held her hands palms out and shrugged. "I don't know that it necessarily means anything. The truth is, I didn't know Maggie very well. I've been feeling a little guilty about her death myself. I was only four years older than her and yet I can't remember ever spending more than four minutes with her."

"You weren't missing much." Lacey's smile turned rueful. "I honestly don't think she was a bad woman. She was just a woman who wanted out of Whisper Cove. She wanted more than this town could provide for her. I'm not happy she thought my husband could be the source of that 'more' she so desperately needed, but now I feel sad that she never had a chance to grow up and learn to provide for herself."

"That's a very good point." Harper shifted her eyes to a group of twenty-somethings standing on the far side of town square. Colin was one of the faces and his eyes brightened when he caught sight of Harper and began flapping his hand in earnest. She managed a smile and waved back, although she felt goofy doing all the while.

"I see Colin is still the president of your fan club," Lacey teased, smirking. "He always has been gaga for you. I thought he might be someone to turn Maggie's fancy for a little bit when they started hanging out but that never came to fruition."

Harper stiffened at the words, surprise washing over her. "Wait ... what are you talking about?"

"Colin and Maggie," Lacey replied, clearly missing the change in Harper's demeanor. "They were hanging out quite a bit in the weeks leading up to her death."

Harper instinctively grabbed Lacey's wrist and forced the woman's attention to fully rest on her. "Are you sure?"

Lacey nodded. "I'm positive. I remember being excited when I saw them hanging out at the ice cream shop about a month ago. They had their heads bent together and were laughing. Even though Maggie was a good two years older than Colin, I thought they might be a decent match because she wasn't very mature."

Harper was dumbfounded. "But ... Colin was with me when we discovered Maggie's body. He said he didn't look at the body so he didn't immediately recognize her, but he didn't say anything about knowing her when Jared and Mel showed up on the scene."

Lacey carefully extricated her wrist from Harper's grip and shrugged. "I don't know what to tell you. I know they were spending time together. There was a big group of kids hanging out – mostly the ones Colin graduated with, mind you – but Heather and Maggie were both hanging out with them, too, along with a few other people. At least that's what I heard around town."

"Huh." Harper's expression turned thoughtful as she watched the boisterous young men entertain each other with what looked to be grandiose tall tales. "Thanks for the information. I need to track down Zander."

"Sure." Lacey offered a mock salute. "I'll try to keep Mikey off your tail since you seem keen to solve a murder. I'm not sure I'll be capable of doing it, though. The kid is like a cat with a spider when he wants to be. He doesn't stop until the spider is missing legs."

"Yeah, well, that's a delightful image."

"Just wait until you have a son. You'll realize I'm telling the truth."

"I'll keep that in mind."


## "SO, WHAT DO YOU THINK?"

It didn't take Harper long to track down Zander. He put up a fight when she dragged him away from his under-aged fan club, but once she launched into the information Lacey had to share he was understandably intrigued.

"Really?" Zander gave Colin a long look with fresh eyes. "Do you think he was putting on an act?"

Harper shrugged. "I don't know. That's the question of the day, though. Do you think he was putting on an act?"

"I've never understood that kid's wide-eyed shtick anyway. I always think he's putting on an act. Now that I know this, though, I can't help but wonder if it's a different act from what I initially envisioned."

"You and me both." Harper was lost in thought as she watched Colin high-five one of his friends. "Do you think I should call Jared?"

"Or you could just wait to tell him at the tour tonight."

"But he might want to follow Colin."

"Colin is registered for the tour," Zander volunteered.

That was news to Harper. "He is?"

"Oh, come on." Zander rolled his eyes. "You know Colin's pattern. He goes on at least three tours every season. He's completely in love with you."

"I didn't realize he was going to be part of the tour tonight," Harper admitted. The news made her uneasy, although she couldn't put her finger on exactly why. "I guess I can wait to tell Jared. We should keep an eye on him for the rest of the afternoon, though."

"If he stays here where the food is, I have no problem with that. If he takes off and forces me to abandon the party before Charlene Dennehy cuts that delicious-looking chocolate cake, I'm totally going to melt down."

"Fair enough. I—" Harper didn't get a chance to finish her statement because a body moved in at her right and caused her to jolt. When she recognized the face that was leering at her, her heart rate increased rather than decreased. Gary Conner always had that effect on her, though. He was a walking advertisement for raised blood pressure. "Hey, Gary."

"Ms. Harlow." Gary didn't look any happier to see Harper and Zander than they were to see him. "Fancy meeting you here."

Harper cocked an eyebrow, confused. "Why is that fancy?"

"Because this isn't a cemetery."

Harper glanced toward Zander for help. "Do you understand what he's saying?"

Zander shook his head. "I haven't understood a word he's said since he showed up for his tour. You're the front man of this operation. I'm leaving you to deal with him."

Harper made a grab for Zander's arm, but he managed to evade her. "Don't you dare leave me, Zander!" she hissed, frustration bubbling up.

"I'll be around," Zander called out. "I'll keep an eye on you know who." He offered an exaggerated wink. "You handle Gary and I'll handle the rest. I think that's a perfect tradeoff."

Harper could think of a few other things to call it. "Zander!"

Zander didn't bother looking over his shoulder and when Harper risked a glance at Gary she found him standing with his arms folded over his chest and an expectant look on his face.

"What do you want?" Harper asked, resigned.

"I want to talk to you about why ghosts aren't real. I've been doing some research about the afterlife and I want to hear your thoughts. I think I finally have information that will convince you I'm right and you've been going about this the wrong way."

Harper was resigned. "Oh, well, I can't wait."

## 12

## TWELVE

Harper and Zander met Molly and Eric in the cemetery parking lot about an hour before dusk. The freshly-minted couple were all smiles as they occasionally locked gazes and readied the equipment, forcing Harper to shake her head as she watched them from across the way.

"Why are you shaking your head like that?" Zander asked, legitimately curious. "Do you see Maggie or something?"

"What? No." Harper reluctantly tore her gaze from Eric and Molly, the latter of whom had dyed her hair bright orange to mark the holiday season. "What do you think when you look at them?"

Zander followed Harper's gaze and shrugged. "I think that I never knew Eric had teeth before he finally started getting some and smiling."

Harper lightly smacked her best friend's forearm. "Don't give him grief. I think they're kind of cute together. I'm just wondering what you think of them."

Zander shrugged as he took in the smiling twosome. "I think they both seem happier than before. I think they're in the honeymoon phase of the relationship and some of that will probably bounce back, but they seem content. I'm happy for them."

Harper smiled. "I'm happy for them, too."

"You're just happy that Eric seems to have forgotten his crush on you and the office is no longer the most uncomfortable place in the world," Zander corrected.

"We're all happy about that," Jared announced, silently moving in behind the two friends and smirking at the way they both jumped. "By the way ... boo." He exhaled on a whisper close to Harper's neck and delighted in the gooseflesh that popped up as he wrapped his arms around her from behind and pressed a soft kiss to the sensitive spot behind her ear. "Hi, Heart."

Harper did her best not to squirm as she shot a pointed look over her shoulder. "You're not supposed to sneak up on the ghost hunters and scare them."

"I didn't realize that was a rule. How come that's outlawed? Is it against the ghost-hunting rules?"

"No, it's just in bad taste." Harper smoothed the front of her shirt before swiveling and giving Jared her full attention. "You're early. I wasn't expecting you for another thirty minutes."

"Well, we ran the names you gave us and came up empty so there wasn't a reason to stay at the office." Jared turned serious as he folded his arms across his chest and leaned against Zander's truck. All five of those kids you mentioned are working and seem to keep their noses out of trouble."

"That doesn't mean one of them isn't hiding something," Harper pointed out. "What did you think about the story Lacey told me?"

"I can't say I'm surprised. That story seems to go hand-in-hand with what Mark Crowley told Mel and me yesterday. Maggie was essentially a young woman who wanted money. I'm guessing she was looking for a way out of Whisper Cove, but I have no confirmation on that. Mel and I are going to have another sit down with Heather now that she's had time to adjust to Maggie's death. She might have thought of something she forgot before."

"So, you think I'm barking up the wrong tree with the tidbit about Maggie and Heather hanging out with Colin's group of friends," Harper mused. "And here I thought I was helping."

"Oh, you helped." Jared slipped a strand of Harper's hair behind her ear. "We needed a place to look, even if it's just to rule out people. You definitely helped. There's nothing odd about those boys that we can find, though. They all seem to have either entry-level or gap jobs and none of them have been arrested or anything."

"That doesn't mean that one of them isn't a psychopath," Zander noted. "Psychopaths are good at hiding their true feelings. One of those kids may be so good that he's bamboozled Whisper Cove's finest into thinking he's an innocent kid minding his own business."

Jared made a face. "And I suppose I'm 'Whisper Cove's finest' in that scenario, huh?"

"You or Mel. It doesn't matter to me. I'm not picky."

Sensing trouble, Harper smoothly stepped between the two men and held her hands up. "No fighting. This is a no-fighting tour. We need to work together if we expect this to work out."

Jared's gaze lingered on Zander a moment longer before he focused on Harper. "No one is going to fight. We're just messing with each other. There's no need to get worked up."

"Yeah, don't get worked up, Harp," Zander teased. "Jared and I had a long talk and agreed that us arguing isn't in your best interests so instead of fighting, from now on, we're going to strip out of our shirts and flex to see who wins when we disagree."

Jared rolled his eyes. "I don't remember agreeing to that."

"You did just to shut me up." Zander's grin was impish. "As for Colin and the others, I don't know that I believe any of them are killers. They seem simple enough, quiet enough, and Colin's crush on you is one of the cutest things I've ever seen."

"I don't know if I would take things that far," Jared hedged. "I think his crush is a little creepy and irritating. That's why I've really looked hard at him. I can't find anything on him, though. There's just nothing there."

"So, we're right back where we started." Harper heaved out a sigh, her lips curving when she heard Molly squeal as Eric gave her a little chase and tickled her ribs. "They're kind of cute, huh?"

"I definitely like them as a couple," Jared replied after a beat. "He's more mature than her, but that's okay. Every relationship needs a calming presence and he's that for them."

Harper knit her eyebrows. "Who is the calming presence in our relationship?"

"Do you even have to ask?"

"I think she does, which is why she asked," Zander offered helpfully, causing Jared to scowl.

"I'm the calming presence in our relationship," Jared explained. "There's nothing wrong with being the excitable one, for the record. That simply means you're the more interesting half of our particular dynamic duo."

"Oh, nice save," Harper muttered, shaking her head. "I'm not sure I agree you're the calm one in our relationship."

All Jared could do was chuckle. "Really? You think you're the calm one in our relationship? How do you figure?"

"I don't know," Harper admitted. "I'm going to need some time to think about it."

"You've got five minutes." Jared flicked his eyes back to Molly and Eric. "I'm just glad he's gotten over his thing for you. I thought I was going to have to beat him up at one point. Now he's so wrapped up in Molly it's not even an issue."

Harper snorted. "Oh, you did not think you were going to have to beat him up."

"I did so. He was always giving me the evil eye even though you were my girlfriend."

Harper was amused despite herself. "He was harmless."

"I believe that's what you said about Colin not twenty-four hours ago," Jared pointed out. "Now you're starting to wonder if he had something to do with Maggie's death. No one is ever truly harmless, Heart. That's why you always need to watch out for yourself."

"I promise to be careful." Harper squeezed his hand. "You don't have to worry about me tonight. It's a haunted cemetery tour. What could possibly go wrong?"

"Ugh." Jared slapped his hand to his forehead, disgusted.

"You totally jinxed us, Harp," Zander complained. "Now something bad is going to happen."

Harper didn't believe in jinxes. "Everything will be fine. Trust me."

**"OH, THIS IS GOING TO BE THE** worst night ever." Harper made a horrified face when she recognized Colin's entire crew loitering in the parking lot waiting for the tour to start almost an hour later. To make matters worse, Gary Conner was back as well and Harper thought for sure she was going to be taken out by a vicious case of heartburn if she was forced to have another philosophical discussion with the repugnant man.

"What happened to your unflagging spirit?" Jared asked as he slung an arm over her shoulders and stared at the men in question. "I'm starting to think this night is going to be even better than I initially envisioned."

Harper slid him a sidelong look, suspicious. "Why do you say that? What do you have planned?"

Jared adopted an innocent expression. "Why do you think I have something planned? I'm just an innocent man completely in love with his girlfriend who just so happens to want to watch her put on a show for her fans. Are you insinuating there's something wrong with that?"

Harper wasn't about to kowtow. "Oh, don't do that. I know you're up to something. I'm going to be watching you to figure out what it is."

"Don't watch me so much you don't pay attention to your tour," Jared teased. "I would hate for your customers to feel ripped off."

"Whatever." Harper zipped her hoodie and frowned. "Why would Gary Conner possibly come back after he hated the last tour so much? In fact, I swear this is like the fifth tour over three or four years that he's been at. It doesn't make sense."

"Maybe it has a little something to do with the tour guide," Jared suggested.

"Or maybe he just likes to complain and this is an easy place for him to have a captive audience," Harper grumbled. "I honestly can't believe I'm going to have to put up with him again."

"You're selling a service," Jared pointed out. "You need to remember that the customer is always right."

Harper snorted. "In this case, the customer is always a tool. Try to keep up on the tour and don't act like my boyfriend the cop. As far as the other guests are concerned, you're just a normal guy enjoying a nice night in the cemetery."

"I'll try to keep that in mind."

"You do that."


**"I'M TELLING YOU** that I did a lot of research and you're wrong. There's no scientific way for ghosts to remain behind and haunt people. It's impossible."

Ten minutes into the tour Harper was already at the point of no return with Gary. The middle-aged man latched onto her the second they set out ... and he hadn't shut up since.

"Gary, I've never pretended to be a scientist." Harper chose her words carefully. "I don't know how some souls stay behind. I just know that they do."

"It's not possible."

"Right." Harper licked her lips and increased her pace, desperate to get away from Gary and his science talk. She had no idea what she was going to focus on, but she imagined she would figure it out as she went along. "So, we're coming up on one of my favorite mausoleums. This is the Burnette mausoleum, and it's home to a rich history ... including a nice old lady who killed off three husbands with knitting needles before getting caught.

"Now, what's interesting about Helen Burnette is not that the husbands she killed are still hanging around, but Helen herself is," she continued. "Before we get into the story of her afterlife, though, we need to talk about her life. It's a long story, but totally interesting."

From the back of the group, Jared smiled as he watched Harper interact with the crowd. Zander remained close – interjecting when necessary – but Jared couldn't help but be impressed by the way Zander stood back and allowed Harper to be the one who shined. He wasn't even sure Zander realized he was doing it, but Jared was beyond grateful for the flamboyant man's giving nature.

"What are you thinking?" Shawn asked, falling into step with Jared.

"I'm thinking that Harper looks really pretty when she tells a ghost story," Jared answered honestly. "I mean ... look at her. She's practically glowing."

Shawn smiled as he focused on Harper's face. "She is. If I didn't know better, I would think she was pregnant because of that glow."

Jared's smile slipped. "Let's not hurry things along before it's necessary, okay? I'd like to enjoy living with her a little bit – perhaps even marrying her – before the talk of babies takes over. I'm not ruling out babies, mind you. It simply isn't something that has to occur right now."

Shawn chuckled, genuinely amused. "I was teasing you. Don't get worked up. I know you guys aren't there yet. I would be a little worried if you were already there, quite frankly. I think things are fine the way they are."

"Yeah?" Jared wasn't convinced. "Have you talked to Zander at all about the changes that are coming? I've wanted to sit him down a few times, but I'm afraid that if I do that he's going to turn it into a big scene and the last thing I want is for Harper to have to play peacemaker between us."

"Zander is ... okay." Shawn surprised himself with his word choice. "He's not exactly what I would call happy about the change, but he understands it's necessary. Zander's biggest problem is that he likes things his way and now that Harper is going to have her own house he recognizes that things will no longer be done to his way of thinking and that's the bitterest pill for him to swallow."

"Is that why he's so adamant we have a pink kitchen?"

Shawn shrugged. "I think he really does like the idea of a pink kitchen and he feels he can't get away with it because it would be stereotypical for us to do it. I mean ... think about it. A gay guy with a pink kitchen is going to get all sorts of guff. Zander doesn't want to be that guy."

"I never even thought about that," Jared admitted. "It's not as creepy when you put it like that. Of course, I'm still not painting the kitchen pink so he's going to have to get over it."

"He will. Give him time." Shawn's smile widened when he watched Zander chime in to Harper's story with sound effects. "They're really quite good. They play off each other well. You can tell they've been at this a long time."

"I think they've been at this since kindergarten," Jared noted, his eyes bouncing over the crowd. "They're definitely entertaining, though. They have everyone focused on them. Our good friend Colin, in fact, is practically drooling as he watches Harper tell her story."

Shawn followed his gaze. "Yeah. He's clearly in love with your girl-friend. I'm guessing you don't like that."

"Would you like that?"

Shawn made a dismissive gesture. "I'm not sure that I would really care. On one hand, it's flattering to see people falling over your mate. It's pure biology that you want the person you choose to be attractive to others because then it validates your choice."

Jared wrinkled his nose. "Are you making that up?"

Shawn chuckled as he shook his head. "It's true. You get validation when others find Harper pretty. I get the same validation when people look at Zander a certain way."

"Yeah, but ... I don't want to share my woman with anyone else so part of me would prefer if no one found her pretty," Jared argued.

"I think you honestly believe that, but it's not true," Shawn countered. "Be honest. If someone told you Harper wasn't pretty, how would you respond?"

"I would tell him he needed his eyes checked."

"Exactly." Shawn crossed his arms over his chest and watched as Colin dreamily followed Harper as she drifted closer to the mausoleum. "He is a little obvious with his adoration, isn't he? I swear he looks as if he's about to drop at her feet and pledge his undying love."

Jared's small smile turned into a pronounced frown. "Is it wrong that I want to beat him up for that even though I know he can't help it and is probably harmless?"

"That's another part of biology," Shawn replied. "As a man, you want to mark your territory."

"Like a dog?"

"If you like. Just don't go over there and lift your leg on Colin. I don't think Harper will like it and she's not going to take biology as an excuse and just let things go."

"Good to know."

"Yeah. I'm a fountain of useless information."

Jared narrowed his eyes as he watched Colin lean closer to one of his comrades and whisper something, the other young man's eyes lighting up as he laughed at whatever Colin said. "Come on. Let's get closer. I want to know what they're talking about."

"Because you want to mark your territory?"

"Because no matter what I told Harper, I can't ignore the fact that Colin was supposedly hanging out with Maggie not long before she was murdered," Jared answered grimly. "I can't help but wonder why he hasn't volunteered that little tidbit yet, especially if he's as innocent as he pretends to be."

"Now that right there is a good reason."

"I thought so."

## 13

# THIRTEEN

Harper was tired after the tour concluded and the last thing she wanted to do was talk to Colin, who strategically placed himself close to Zander's vehicle and left her no option but to talk to him or flee. He was bending Shawn's ear at the moment, something she hoped he would get tired of, so she ducked behind a nearby storage building to catch her breath.

The tour went well. She had no complaints about that. Some of the attending faces were familiar, but many were new and Harper always loved seeing the wonder on a new fan's face. There was joy in the telling of the same old stories when you had fresh faces in the mix. Of course, the fact that Colin and his crew attended set Harper's teeth on edge – even though she couldn't exactly say why – and Gary was turning into a real pill. She had no idea why the man insisted on attending a ghost tour when he wasn't a believer, but Harper was starting to think that it was because he wanted to be right. There was a desperate need in the man to turn Harper to his way of thinking ... and she couldn't wrap her head around why he was so desperate to change her mind when it came to an enduring human spirit.

To settle her heart and mind, Harper kept her back to the building – the cemetery's ground crews kept lawnmowers, rakes, fertilizer and the like inside – and shut her eyes as she sucked in steady breaths to calm herself. Gary was annoying, but it wasn't as if he was capable of shaking her belief system. Harper knew who she was. She was well aware of what she could do. That wouldn't change.

As if on cue, Harper felt a burning gaze on her and slowly returned to reality. When she opened her eyes, she found Maggie's ghost standing about twenty feet away. The ethereal woman was staring, and she didn't look happy.

"Well, I guess that answers that question," Harper muttered as she pushed herself away from the brick wall, being careful to keep her voice low in case any of the tour guests decided to come looking for her. "I knew I saw you."

"You're the ghost woman." Maggie's comment was simple, matter-of-fact. "I always thought what they said about you was a bunch of crap but now ... well ... not so much."

"I *am* the ghost woman," Harper agreed, looking the weary woman up and down. She wore the same outfit Harper recognized from when Maggie's body was discovered, although the shirt looked different. It was bright, probably because of the Halloween party she attended before her death. "What was your costume?"

"I didn't really have a costume. I just wanted to look pretty."

"Right. To meet a rich man?"

Maggie narrowed her eyes. "Who have you been talking to?"

Since Harper wasn't familiar with Maggie's personality in life, she decided to dive in feet first and see if she could tread water with the persnickety ghost rather than beat around the bush now that one of them was mired in a traumatic death. She figured feeling her way around would be quicker than playing games. "Everyone pretty much said the same thing about you. Apparently you were looking for a rich guy to fund your shopping habits and maybe even get you out of Whisper Cove. Is that what you were looking for?"

"Who doesn't want out of Whisper Cove?"

Harper raised her hand. "I happen to like Whisper Cove. I don't ever want to leave. I like it here. I've always liked it here, though. I guess it's probably different for those who want to be close to a bigger city.

"Still, it's not as if you're out in the middle of nowhere here," she continued. "You're within thirty minutes of bigger cities and malls. That's not so bad."

"It's not good either." Maggie floated a bit closer. "I don't understand why I'm here. I mean ... I get that I'm dead. I knew the second I woke up in this ... hell hole ... that I was dead, and that was before I tried to find my phone in my pants and realized my fingers kept disappearing into my butt."

Harper made a face at the mental picture Maggie painted. "Nice. Um ... I want to help you – despite the fact that I just know I'm going to have nightmares about trying to grab my cell phone later – but I'm going to need more information to work with. What can you tell me about that night at the barn party?"

"There's not much to tell. I got dressed up, headed there with Heather, talked to a bunch of a people and then ... nothing. I don't remember what happened after that. It's not even a blur. It's darkness."

Maggie was the morose sort and it took everything Harper had not to comment on her attitude. "What about Colin? I understand you were hanging around with his group."

"Colin?" Maggie screwed up her face in concentration. "Are you talking about Colin Thompson? Why are you asking about him?"

"Because I heard he was at the party with you. I heard you guys were spending time together. He was also tagging along on my tour the night we found you. That's a little too coincidental for me to ignore."

"Who told you I was spending time with Colin?"

"Lacey Kaiser."

"Ugh." Maggie's distaste was obvious as she shook her head. "I should've figured. She's been out to get me for weeks. Actually, it's more like months."

"Out to get you? How?"

"Um ... she called the police on me two weeks ago and told them I was driving drunk. If that's not being out to get me, I don't know what is."

Harper was understandably confused. "I'm not sure I understand. Lacey called which cops to report you for drunk driving?"

"It wasn't the locals, so don't bother asking your boy toy," Maggie sneered. "He's hot and I thought about going after him, by the way, but then I found out what a cop makes and I ruled that out."

Harper was disgusted by Maggie's attitude. "I like how you just assume that you could've snagged Jared."

"I like how you assume I couldn't." Maggie was clearly spoiling for a fight. "It doesn't really matter now, does it? I'm dead and your boyfriend is free from my clutches."

"You are dead," Harper agreed, tugging on her limited patience. "The thing is, I still want to help you despite how obnoxious you're being. I need to know what happened to you."

"I don't remember what happened to me. I already told you that."

Harper pictured the dreamscape from the previous night. "Were you chased in the woods? Did you drive yourself here after the party? Were you with someone? I need you to think."

"And I can't think because there's nothing there!" Maggie exploded. "I don't remember. I've been trying to remember since I woke on the ground by a freaking tombstone, but there's nothing there. I just ... why are you pushing me?"

"Because I want to solve the mystery of your death and help you cross over," Harper replied honestly. "I don't think hanging around here is going to help your attitude."

"And I don't think you can help me." Maggie made a show of moving her foot, as if she were scuffing it against the ground, perhaps a nervous habit carried over from life. "I don't even know why I followed you. There's nothing more for me than this."

"That's not true. There's more out there."

"How would you know?"

"I've ... seen it." Harper didn't know how to explain the flashes of the other side she'd witnessed. The only thing she did know was that those flashes left her feeling content, warm all over. "You can have something better than this, Maggie. Sure, you can't have what you thought you were going to get out of life, but that doesn't mean this is it."

"I think it is." Maggie turned in the opposite direction and headed toward the woods. Harper noted that she was moving away from the area where her body was discovered and found that odd.

"I can help you," Harper called out.

"I don't think you can, but you need to worry about yourself more than me. I can't die twice. There's someone watching you from the trees on the other side of that building. Over there." Maggie vaguely waved as she departed. "I would be careful because ... well ... I'm not getting a very good vibe off him. Perhaps you'll be joining me in this terrible place after all."

Harper jerked her head to the left and stared hard at the trees, which suddenly felt larger than life and intimidating. She clasped her hands together and took a step away from the wall, hoping the increased distance between her and the light on the corner of the small brick building would allow her to make out a form in the trees.

She didn't immediately see anyone ... but she sensed someone close.

"Who is there?" Harper did her best to appear brave as she gazed into the darkness.

No one responded, but Harper was almost positive she heard the rustle of fallen leaves and it made her blood run cold as the hair on the back of her neck stood on end.

"Who is it?" Harper repeated, taking a step away from the sound. She was technically moving away from Jared, Zander, and Shawn, but that somehow felt safer than plunging into the woods and trying to outrun whoever was there.

No one answered again and Harper essentially forgot to breathe when she sensed someone staring at her. She imagined she could hear whoever it was breathing even though she knew that to be ridiculous.

Harper's voice was barely a whisper when she spoke again. "Who are you?"

This time Harper saw a hint of movement, but she didn't get a chance to stare hard enough to make out features because Jared picked that moment to come looking for her.

"Harper?"

She heard him call out and moved her eyes slightly to the right as she looked for his familiar face. She didn't see him immediately, and when she looked to the left again, the shadow she saw before was gone.

She almost believed she'd imagined it because the spot was so wide open and empty.

Harper finally managed to breathe as Jared stepped into her vision field and she rested her hands on her knees as she sucked in gaping mouthfuls of oxygen.

"What's going on?" Jared asked, instantly alert. "What happened?"

"I want to go home," Harper replied without hesitation. "I just ... want to go home."

Jared held out his hand, worry coursing through him even as he scanned the area for an interloper ... to no avail. "Then we'll go home. Come on. I'll get you out of here right now."


**JARED FILLED A BATHTUB** with hot water and a fragrant bath bomb before leaving Harper in the bathroom by herself to soak. He joined Zander and Shawn in the living room shortly after they returned to the house, thankful for their presence and steady camaraderie. All three men sensed something was up with Harper, although none of them seemed to agree on what that something was.

"How is she?" Shawn asked, handing Jared a beer as the weary police officer sank into the chair at the end of the room. "She seemed quiet when you brought her back to the parking lot after the tour."

"She *was* quiet." Jared took a long drag on his beer before continuing. "She was also a little shaky."

"Did she say anything to you?"

"She said that she saw Maggie's ghost and the woman is unfriendly and she doesn't like her," Jared replied. "She also said that Maggie doesn't remember what happened to her."

"That can't be the only thing that happened," Zander argued. "She was more upset than that when she came back."

"I would agree with you there," Jared said. "She didn't say a lot for the ride home, but she finally opened up a little bit when I was getting the bath ready. I could tell she didn't want to share, but I reminded her that we're a couple and that means telling each other the truth."

"So, what did she say?"

"She said that Maggie announced someone was watching from the trees," Jared replied. "Harper says she can't be sure, but she's almost positive she felt someone there, right in the spot Maggie indicated, watching her."

Zander leaned forward, somber. "Why didn't she yell for help?"

"I guess she was still debating what to do. She said she didn't want to make a scene if it was just one of the people from the tour because she thought it would ruin her street cred."

Shawn snorted. "Only Harper would say something like that after being spooked in a cemetery."

"Exactly, right?" Jared took another drink. "I'm trying to remember who was in the parking lot when I went looking for her. Do you guys remember?"

"Um, not really," Shawn said after a beat. "I didn't pay attention to the faces before that, though. I was more interested in watching the Harper and Zander Show. I would be lying if I said otherwise."

"The Zander and Harper Show," Zander automatically corrected, cocking a challenging eyebrow when Jared shot him a look. "What? We all know I would be the lead if Harper and I had our own show."

Jared made a dismissive sound in the back of his throat. "Anyway, back to the topic at hand. Harper tried to play it off and say she was probably imagining things because Maggie put the idea in her head, but I can't shake the idea that maybe someone was out there watching her."

"Why do you say that?" Shawn asked. "I mean ... who would be watching her?"

"It could've been anyone. Colin and his group were there and I'm giving serious thought to isolating him and asking some questions tomorrow. If he knows who killed Maggie, he might be willing to talk to save himself."

"What if he's the one who killed Maggie?" Shawn pressed.

Zander held up his hand to garner attention before Jared could answer. "Listen, I'm not going to pretend Colin isn't annoying, but I swear he's harmless," Zander said. "We've known that kid for years ... and I mean freaking years. He's been hot to trot for Harp since the start. That doesn't make him a murderer."

"I didn't say he was a murderer," Jared snapped. "He might know something, though. He was hanging around Maggie and didn't volunteer that information. That strikes me as odd."

"He was also on the tour tonight and hanging around with me toward the end," Shawn added. "I think he thought he might get a chance to talk to Harper if he stuck close. She disappeared, though."

"That's right." Jared bobbed his head. "You were talking to Colin. How long was he bugging you next to the truck?"

Shawn held his hands palms out and shrugged. "I don't know. Ten minutes, I guess. At a certain point, I think he realized Harper wasn't going to come over and he made a break for it. That was a few minutes before you said you were going to find Harper."

"Where did Colin go after he broke away from you?" Jared asked. "Did he leave with his friends? Did he head into the woods?"

"I ... don't know." Shawn felt helpless. "I wasn't paying attention. I was just glad he stopped talking because he was being ridiculously annoying."

"That kid is always annoying," Zander muttered. "That doesn't mean he's a murderer, though."

"I didn't say he was a murderer," Jared stressed. "That doesn't mean I'm not worried about Harper. She's not the type to let her imagination get away from her. If she believes someone was watching her from the woods, I have to believe that's true."

"I would probably agree with that, too," Shawn said. "How do you want to handle her safety going forward?"

"I don't want her alone if we can help it. She spends most of her days with Zander, which is good, but he can't watch her every moment during tours. He's just as busy as she is sometimes, and they still have a tour or two to finish out the week."

"So, what?" Zander asked. "Are you going on every tour with us until they're over?"

"As long as I can manage it. I'm not leaving Harper to fend for herself if I can help it. I'm not built that way."

"I'll clear my schedule and make sure I can be there for the remaining tours, too," Shawn offered. "It won't take much. I'll just work day shifts at the gym and give everyone else the night shifts. That's one of the perks of being the boss."

"Thanks." Jared couldn't help being relieved. "Just knowing an extra set of eyes will be on her makes me feel better."

"What about you?" Zander asked. "What are you going to do?"

"The first thing I'm going to do is drag Colin Thompson in for questioning tomorrow," Jared replied. "After that, I have no idea. We're nowhere near as close to solving this case as I would like and I can't help but feel that time is of the essence here."

"Why do you think that?" Shawn was legitimately curious. "Honestly, why do you think you're running out of time?"

"Because I can't shake the idea that whoever killed Maggie isn't done," Jared replied. "No matter what happens, I'm going to make sure that he doesn't finish up with Harper. I won't be able to live with it if I overlook something and she pays the price."

"None of us will," Shawn said. "Don't worry. You can count on us."

"I hope so. I certainly can't do it alone."

"You can count on me, too," Zander offered. "In fact, the only thanks I ask in return is that you paint your kitchen pink. I think we'll be all squared up after that."

Jared scowled. "You need to let that go."

"Never."

"You make me so tired sometimes."

"Pink would perk you right up."

"Cripes. I need another beer."

## 14

# FOURTEEN

Harper did her best not to toss and turn in an effort to let Jared sleep. She slumbered intermittently, marking an hour at the most before waking again, and when she climbed out of bed the next morning she was even more exhausted than when she initially rested her head on the pillow.

"Are you feeling okay?" Jared pressed his hand to Harper's forehead before she could answer. "You don't feel warm, but you look sick."

Harper mustered a smile that didn't make it all the way to her eyes. "I'm not quite sure how to take that. Not all of us can wake looking as good as you. Some of us have bedhead to deal with."

"I happen to like the bedhead." Jared pressed a kiss against her forehead before pulling back. "You didn't sleep, did you?"

"I was right next to you. I slept."

"Not well."

"I still slept. You don't need to worry about me." Harper squeezed his wrist. "I'm sure I'll feel better after a shower. Hopefully for you, I'll look better, too."

Jared made a rueful face. "That's going to come back to bite me, isn't it?"

"Probably."

"I still don't think you got enough sleep," he muttered as he followed her toward the bathroom. "We're going to talk about this over breakfast."

"I can't wait."

## "YOU LOOK LIKE CRAP."

Zander made a face thirty minutes later as he doled out eggs, hash browns, and bacon onto Harper's plate. Shawn slid a glass of juice in front of her and pointedly elbowed Zander before sitting next to Harper.

"I think you look fantastic," Shawn countered. "In fact, I think you look like an absolute dream. You could be a model or something."

Harper arched an eyebrow. "That was laying it on a bit thick."

Shawn was sheepish. "I knew it as soon as I said it. You are really pretty, though."

For the first time all morning, Harper managed a legitimate smile. "Thank you."

"Oh, when *he* says it you believe him," Jared groused as he sat on Harper's other side.

"I believe it when you say it most of the time, too," Harper shot back. "I simply don't believe it five minutes after you tell me I look like crap warmed over twice."

"I'm fairly certain I said nothing of the sort." Jared tapped the side of Harper's plate. "You need to eat this. You still look sick."

"Right. I look sick, not like crap warmed over twice."

"You guys seem like you're in great frames of mind this morning," Zander noted as he deposited a plate of toast on the table before taking the final seat. "Are you fighting? Please tell me it's because Harper has finally come to her senses and agreed to my pink kitchen project and you're taking it as a dagger to the heart, Jared."

"Neither one of us is ever going to come to your way of thinking on that one," Jared shot back. "As for my very beautiful but tired girl-friend, I think you should cancel whatever you guys have going today and enjoy some serious resting."

Whatever response he was expecting, that wasn't it. Zander furrowed his brow. "You want us to spend the day resting?"

Jared nodded. "I think you guys should sit around in your pajamas, eat candy, and watch however many chick flicks you can stomach."

Now it was Harper's turn to make a face. "It's Halloween. We don't watch chick flicks during Halloween."

"First of all, assuming I sit around and watch chick flicks all day is stereotypical and I don't like it," Zander complained.

Jared held up his hands in capitulation. "I'm sorry."

"You're forgiven, but only because I happen to be a fan of chick flicks at all times. Harper's not wrong, though," Zander supplied. "October is horror movie month. December is Lifetime Christmas movie month."

"And old episodes of *Little House on the Prairie* so we can cry without guilt," Harper added.

Zander extended a finger and smirked. "And that. February is romance month. May is for animated movies. September is for alien movies. Um ... what am I forgetting, Harp?"

"June."

"Right. June is for *Gossip Girl* reruns."

Jared was dumbfounded. "I've been practically living with you guys for months. How can I not know this?"

"We don't broadcast our idiosyncrasies," Harper replied. "We feel if we let too many of our secrets slip, no one will ever love us."

Jared rolled his eyes. "Wow. I don't even know what to say to that. I'm looking forward to September, though. I happen to love Sigourney Weaver."

Shawn shot him an enthusiastic thumbs-up. "Right on. Why *Gossip Girl*, though?"

"Because Chuck and Blair are awesome," Zander replied. "I'm also a big fan of headbands and I don't think women wear them enough. Plus, I mean ... Lonely Boy turned out to be Gossip Girl. There's irony there. I'm sure of it. I happen to love irony."

"Fair enough."

"Okay, we're going to discuss this monthly movie schedule thing later," Jared said. "For now, though, why can't you guys take the day off and watch horror movies? It's almost Halloween. You guys have been running yourselves ragged for weeks. Take a breather."

"I think you're just saying that because you want me out of harm's way." Harper mixed her eggs and hash browns together, adding salt and pepper to the mix before forking some onto a slice of toast. "I already told you that I'm not really sure if someone was there last night. Besides that, even if someone was there, we don't know that it was just some random visitor or a tour guest."

"You know," Jared argued. "You felt afraid. You have good instincts. Don't turn your back on them now."

"Oh, that's very sweet."

Jared made a face as she bit into her weird breakfast concoction. "What are you doing?"

"It's our version of a breakfast bowl," Zander explained. "Don't judge her for it. I made it for the first time when we were in middle school. It's comfort food."

"How did you know she would need comfort this morning?" Jared asked.

"Because I figured she would have a rough time sleeping. It turns out I was right." Zander mixed his food together in the same manner as Harper. "I'm also right about the pink kitchen."

"Don't push me on that." Jared was at his limit. "Heart, I just think you should take it easy today. I know I would feel better if you did."

"How about we compromise?" Harper suggested. "What if Zander and I agree to spend the morning here resting and watching bad horror movies ... ."

"I totally want to watch *Ghost Ship*," Zander enthused.

Harper nodded. "And we promise to hold off from doing anything until after we all meet and compare notes over lunch."

Jared was caught off guard by the suggestion. "Where do you want to meet?"

"Jason's restaurant. He has pumpkin soup today. I know because he texted me yesterday to say he was going to have it. I happen to love pumpkin soup."

Jared shoveled a forkful of eggs into his mouth to give himself time to consider the suggestion. He started nodding before finishing swallowing. "Okay. I want to talk to Colin Thompson. I also want to know you're safe and resting this morning. I agree to your terms."

Harper smiled. "Great."

"I want you to try to rest, though."

"I will."

"I also want to make April action adventure month," Jared added. "I want to play, too."

Harper snickered as she briefly leaned her head against his shoulder. "I can live with that."

**MEL AND JARED HAD AN** interrogation room ready when Colin showed up. They sent an officer to pick up the young man at his house, apparently catching him while eating his Fruity Pebbles, and strategically placed themselves in the room as they waited for him to arrive.

By the time Colin walked into the interrogation room, he was a nervous wreck. That was exactly what Jared was going for, even though Mel thought he was taking things too far. Jared took the spot at the head of the table and watched as Colin picked a chair a decent way down on the far side. Jared found it interesting that he wanted to keep distance between them. Of course, that didn't necessarily mean anything.

"Thank you for coming in, Colin." Jared purposely kept his voice authoritative and detached. "I'm sorry if you had other plans, but we feel this is urgent and cannot wait."

"I'm off for the day, but I didn't get the idea that I had a lot of choice about coming." Colin's hands shook as he rested them on the table. "I don't understand why I'm here. I ... didn't do anything."

"Are you sure about that?"

"I think so."

"But you don't know?"

"I ... why am I here?" Colin sounded pathetic and whiny, but he didn't seem to notice. "I know I didn't do anything bad enough to get dragged in here."

"That's still to be ascertained." Jared made a big show of shuffling papers in the folder in front of him. "We have a few things to talk about. Where do you think we should start?"

"I have no idea. I don't even know why you want to talk to me. Unless ... ." Colin broke off and tilted his head to the side. "Is this about Harper?"

Jared managed to keep from flinching at mention of his girlfriend's name. "Why do you think this is about Harper?"

"Because you're her boyfriend."

"And what is she to you?"

"She's ... awesome." Colin took on a far-off expression. "She's so pretty and fun. She can see ghosts ... and talk to them ... and she's always ready for an adventure. She looks really good in her jeans, too. I mean ... like really good. Her butt kind of looks like an apple, which makes me want to take a bite out of it."

Colin realized what he was saying and his cheeks flushed with color as he darted a look to Jared. For his part, the police officer managed to hold it together – even as Mel's shoulders shook with silent laughter – but just barely.

"What was I saying again?" Colin asked, licking his lips.

"I believe you were talking about how Jared's girlfriend is an apple-bottomed girl," Mel offered.

"We're not talking about that," Jared said hurriedly. "We're going to talk about something else. We'll start with your relationship with Maggie Harris. What can you tell me about that?"

"Maggie?" Colin wrinkled his forehead. "I didn't really know Maggie."

"That's not what others have told us. We heard you and your friends were hanging around with Maggie and Heather for weeks before Maggie's murder. I couldn't help but notice you didn't mention that when you found out who Gary Conner tripped over the other night."

"That's because I didn't think it was important," Colin supplied. "It's not as if we were friends. We were just hanging around the same people. She was much more interested in Jay's group than our group. She only tolerated us because she wanted to be close to Jay, and Jay and I hung around occasionally because we graduated together."

Mel stretched his long legs out under the table and crossed them at the ankles. "Are you talking about Jay Forrester?"

"Who is Jay Forrester?" Jared asked.

"He was quarterback of the football team, the most popular kid in school the year that Colin graduated. Last time I heard, he was selling cars at that place his father owns out on Hall Road."

"That's the Jay I'm talking about," Colin confirmed. "He hangs at Dave & Buster's four nights a week. We meet him there for game night at least once a week, sometimes twice if we're really bored. It's not a big deal."

"And how did Maggie play into this?" Jared was starting to get the sinking suspicion that Colin wasn't as dark and demented as he initially thought. There was every possibility that Colin was simply a geeky kid who spent far too much time looking at Harper's rear end.

"Maggie started showing up a couple of weeks ago and I couldn't figure out why at first because she really seemed like an unhappy person," Colin replied. "I don't want to speak ill of the dead but ... she was a total witch with a capital W."

It took everything Jared had not to start laughing. It was a surreal situation, but Colin's reaction somehow struck him as funny. "I'm going to need more information than that. How was she a witch?"

"She was just rude all the time. It was as if she decided that some people were worth talking to and others were not only a waste of time but also something to make fun of because she got off on being mean to people."

"Let me guess, she was nice to the people with money and mean to the ones still living in their parents' basements."

"Pretty much," Colin agreed. "How did you know that?"

"Let's just say that Maggie had a certain reputation," Jared replied. "She only wanted to associate herself with people who had money. You just said this Jay guy was working at his father's car lot, though. That doesn't suggest to me that he had a lot of money."

"Maggie didn't realize that until two weeks ago, though," Colin said. "Up until then she thought Jay had money because he was always flashing a wad of bills. She didn't know he stole that money from his dad's safe."

"Wait a second." Mel held up his hand and leaned forward. "Are you saying Jay Forrester stole from his father?"

"I'm saying that's the rumor and his dad changed the combination on the safe so Jay ran out of money. When that happened, Maggie was irritated. She kept asking questions and not getting the answers she wanted."

"And yet she still hung around," Jared noted. "If she was really that irritated, why did she hang around?"

"Probably because Jay suggested a way for them both to make money and Maggie jumped at it," Colin replied. "I thought she would call him crazy and run away, but she was all for it. All I know is that I didn't want to be part of it so I backed away. Actually, my entire little group backed away because we were all afraid they were going to do something stupid and maybe drag us into it."

Jared was officially intrigued. "So, Jay suggested a new plan of action to Maggie where they could both make money? I'm dying to know what that is."

"They were going to rob the bank."

Jared felt as if Colin had kicked his legs out from under him. "I'm sorry but ... what?"

"They were going to rob the bank," Colin repeated. "I don't mean that they were going to take guns and hold it up or anything. They were going to do a heist ... like in *Ocean's Eleven* ... and steal everything in the vault and make a run for it."

Colin was calm as he offered up the information.

"Seriously, I'm not making it up. True story."

Jared slowly flicked his eyes to Mel. "I think we might have finally got that little tidbit we needed to start narrowing this down."

Mel nodded. "I'm right there with you. Things are finally getting interesting."

# FIFTEEN

Jared texted he was going to be a few minutes late so Harper and
Zander chose a cozy booth in the corner of Jason Thurman's
beachside restaurant, both reaching for the specials menu at the
center of the table at the same time.

"I saw it first," Zander growled, jerking the menu away and pinning
Harper with a dark look.

"What's going on here?" Jason asked, taken aback as he carried
mugs of something that smelled delicious toward the table.

"What is that?" Harper asked, leaning forward. "It smells
heavenly."

"Pumpkin coffee delight." Jason beamed at her, his smile slipping
after a moment's contemplation. "You look tired."

"Oh, geez." Harper rolled her eyes as Zander cackled delightedly
and studied the specials menu. "Do I have a neon sign over my head
flashing 'didn't get enough sleep last night' or something? What is it
with you people saying I look tired? Don't you know that's an insult?"

Jason shrugged as he placed the pumpkin coffee on the table. "You
look tired. I can't help but worry about you. I'm still hoping you're
going to give up your cop and come running back to me."

"I thought we agreed you were going to stop flirting with my woman," Jared said, taking Jason by surprise when he appeared at his left side and slid around the gregarious restaurant owner so he could take his rightful spot next to Harper. "Hey, Heart. How are you feeling?" He slid a strand of her hair behind her ear as he studied her face. "Did you sleep at all?"

Harper let loose an exaggerated sigh as she rolled her eyes. "Apparently I should be walking around with a bag over my head."

"That's not what I said and you know it," Jared said. "You look tired, though, and I'm not going to pretend otherwise. I thought you were going to nap."

"No, I said I would relax. We watched horror movies all morning, per your instructions, and lounged around and did nothing else."

"Right." Jared gave her a quick kiss on the cheek before wrinkling his nose and inhaling deeply. "What is that?"

"Oh, now you're interested," Jason drawled. He had something of a combative relationship with Jared since he returned to town with hopes of rekindling an old high school romance with Harper. Since Jared was already firmly entrenched in her life, that didn't happen. That didn't mean they didn't poke and prod one another on a regular basis when the mood struck. "It's my own personal experiment. I call it pumpkin delight."

"Well, it smells delightful," Jared drawled as he slid out of his coat and draped his arm over Harper's shoulders. "Lay it on me."

"Whatever." Jason made a face but disappeared to do Jared's bidding.

"How are you really?" Jared asked, tipping Harper's chin so he could better see her face. "You're awfully pale."

Harper slapped away Jared's hand when he moved to trace the dark circles under her eyes. "I'm not sick. Stop treating me like I'm fragile because I'm not fragile. I'm not suddenly going to break because I had one restless night."

"Fine. You're not fragile." Jared held up his hands in mock defeat as Jason returned with his pumpkin delight. "Come to papa." Jared grinned as he accepted the mug and sipped. "Wow. That really is delightful. If you weren't constantly hitting on my woman I might spend more time with you just so I could drink this."

Harper cocked an eyebrow. "You know I hate it when you refer to me as your woman, right?"

Jared nodded. "It's man thing, Heart. I can't stop myself. You'll have to learn to live with it."

"That's why you should paint your kitchen pink," Zander offered helpfully. "You could teach him a lesson about thinking of you as property while creating a warm environment to cook all his meals in once you guys are living in domestic bliss."

Jared blinked several times in rapid succession. "What did you just say?"

"Ignore him." Harper patted his wrist. "I'm not going to paint our new kitchen pink. You don't have to worry about that."

"What new kitchen?" Jason asked, shifting from one foot to the other so he could study faces. "I think I'm behind a little bit."

Zander's face lit with glee when he realized Jason wasn't up on the gossip. He had a rather dour relationship with Jason, too, although it was improving. "Oh, you haven't heard, huh?"

Jason's face was blank. "Heard what?"

"Harper and Jared are moving in together." It took everything Zander had to not tip his hand and show Jason his glee. "They are officially going to be homeowners together in a few weeks."

"Technically we're already homeowners together now," Jared pointed out. "We closed quickly because Carol wanted to unload the house. We're simply not moving in for a few weeks."

"Which means I still have a shot of convincing you to paint the house pink," Zander mused.

"We're not painting anything pink!" Jared snapped.

"Actually, I thought we might paint that tiny bathroom off the mudroom pink," Harper hedged. "It's small and pink will brighten up the space. If you don't like that idea, though, we can go with something else."

Jared faltered. He wanted Harper to have what she wanted and he doubted very much he would ever use that bathroom. Of course, he also didn't want Zander to think he'd won. "Um ... ."

"Think about it." Harper patted Jared's knee. "So, I want some of that pumpkin soup you mentioned over the phone, Jason. I also want a grilled cheese and a salad. Apparently I need to eat more vegetables so people will stop telling me I look tired."

Jason barely absorbed Harper's order because he was too busy staring at Jared. "You guys are moving in together?"

Jared met Jason's gaze with an even one of his own. "We are. We bought the house across the road so Harper can still be close to Zander and I won't have to worry about her being alone and bored on nights I have to work late."

"We also have more riverfront land," Harper added. "We're going to put up a new hammock and everything."

Jared's grin was lazy. "We're definitely doing that. I can't wait until we can hammock again."

Jason was lost in thought. "You know the word hammock isn't a verb, right?"

"It is the way we do it." Jared studied Jason's face for a long beat. Even though he was annoyed when the man first returned to town they'd come to something of an uneasy truce. Jason promised to respect Harper's relationship with Jared. In return, Jared promised to stop gracing Jason with threatening glares. It was an uneasy truce but a truce all the same.

"I can't believe you guys are moving in together." Jason exhaled heavily as he sat in the nearest chair at an empty table across the aisle. "This sucks."

"Well, thank you so much for that," Jared deadpanned. "I thought it was a fun way for us to get some privacy and still keep Harper close to Zander. It was the perfect solution for everybody involved."

"Even though they won't let me pick paint colors," Zander groused.

"And that's not going to change," Jared fired back. "This is Harper's house. She gets to pick paint colors."

"Don't you want to pick them with me?" Harper queried.

Jared shrugged. "I want you to be happy. If you want to pick the paint colors, I'm fine with that. Just ... no pink. I'm also not a big fan of orange."

"Duly noted." Harper traced Jared's fingers as she watched Jason for signs of life. He seemed lost in thought. "Are you going to be trapped in your own head over there for a long time? I really wanted some of that pumpkin soup."

"I'm not trapped in my head." Jason recovered quickly. "I just ... I can't believe you're moving in together. I guess that means I really don't have a shot, huh?"

Jared narrowed his eyes. "I thought we agreed that was the case months ago. Are you telling me you thought you had a shot with Harper despite that long conversation we had?"

"I thought as long as she didn't have a ring on her finger there was a chance you guys might break up, which would allow me to swoop in." Jason opted for honesty. "I guess that's not the case, though."

"Oh, they're not getting married," Zander countered. "They're just living in sin."

"You're not getting married?" Jason furrowed his brow. "How come?"

The question caught Jared off guard. "I ... you ... what?"

"Why aren't you getting married?" Jason repeated. "I would think that's the natural next step for you guys, even before you share a roof."

"Um ... ." Harper's cheeks burned under Jason's scrutiny. She hadn't given marriage much thought when Jared suggested moving in together. It didn't seem necessary. Now, in the face of Jason's simple query, she didn't have an answer and that made her feel conflicted. "I ... don't know. He didn't ask. It's not a big deal."

"It's not a big deal?" Jason's eyebrows migrated north on his forehead. "How come it's not a big deal?" He turned to Jared. "How come you don't want to marry her?"

"Yeah. How come you don't want to marry her?" Zander echoed. "I didn't really think about it all that much when you started talking about moving, but marriage would make sense. You guys have been together for months now."

Jared's mouth went dry. "Who wants to hear about the information I got from Colin Thompson this morning? Anyone? It's good information."

"I want to know why you didn't propose to Harper," Zander pressed. "Do you think she's not good enough to propose to or something? I'll have you know, you would be lucky to be married to a woman like her. I mean ... how can you not think she's good enough to marry?"

Jared was completely and totally flabbergasted. He had no idea how the conversation had taken such a turn − and he wasn't comfortable with it in the least. He was determined to get it back on track. "Let's talk about Colin."

"I would totally marry you, Harper," Jason offered. "There's still time to make the right choice."

"Knock that off," Jared hissed, extending a warning finger as his composure broke. "We're going to get married so just ... back off."

"We're getting married?" Harper couldn't hide her surprise. "When did that happen?"

"It hasn't happened yet," Jared replied.

"But it's going to happen soon?" Zander pressed.

"It's going to happen when it's the right time," Jared gritted out, his frustration threatening to overwhelm him. "Listen, moving in together was something I entertained in the back of my mind until the house became available. It was something that I thought was still a bit down the line because I knew Harper wasn't ready to leave Zander.

"Then the perfect house opened up and I jumped on it," he continued. "That house solved so many problems. It was as if it was meant to be."

"That's great about the house," Jason intoned. "What about marrying Harper, though? I would think that would go hand in hand."

Jared scowled. "I cannot believe I'm having this conversation with an audience," he muttered.

"You don't need to explain yourself." Harper's lips curved as she patted his hand. "There's no reason to get upset. You're not ready to get married. I'm okay with that."

"You are?"

"I think things are good between us and I'm happy," Harper replied without hesitation. "There's no need to push yourself to do something you're not ready to do simply because we're moving in together.

"You're right about that house being perfect for us," she continued. "I knew that our living arrangements couldn't stay the same if I expected everyone to remain happy ... and there was a very real chance you and Shawn would end up unhappy if something wasn't done.

"I'm not going to lie. I was worried about that," Harper said. "Then the house opened up and you came up with the perfect solution. I don't need to be married on top of that. I have everything I want right now. It's fine."

Jared stared into the fathomless depths of her eyes and made a tsking sound in the back of his throat. "Heart, I hate it that you just said that."

Harper couldn't hide her mirth. "Would you rather that I be angry and snap at you?"

Jared nodded. "Yeah." He grabbed her hand and squeezed. "Truth be told, I didn't really think about marriage when I landed on the idea of buying the house. Once I realized it was going to be up for sale, that's all I could focus on until the deed was done."

"You don't have to apologize to me."

"No, I think I do. I just wish I didn't have to do it in front of these two pains in my behind." Jared raised his hand so he could block Zander's keen stare. "As for marriage, we haven't even been dating for a year yet. I do see that happening for us, but I haven't planned anything yet. I don't want to lie and say that I have."

"I'm not expecting a proposal." Harper was firm. "If you never propose ... well ... I would rather be happy."

"See, I wish you would be more demanding sometimes. You're too easy to get along with on that front." Jared shifted on the booth seat to get more comfortable. "I see marriage in our future. I just haven't had a chance to give it a lot of thought, and I don't see that changing until after we're moved in and settled.

"The thing is, I want to give you everything that I possibly can because you deserve it and I'm just now realizing that perhaps I went about things a little backward," he continued. "I didn't want to miss that house and I let it cloud things a bit. I'm sorry about that."

"I'm not." Harper was earnest. "We're okay. You don't have to apologize."

"I know that. I just want you to know that I'm not discarding marriage. I am going to get us there, after we paint the new house ...

and move in to the new house ... and celebrate our first Christmas together ... and make sure you're safe from whoever is out there trying to hurt people."

Harper grinned. "I know. It's okay."

"It's not, but I'll get us there." Jared refused to back down. "I want it to be special ... and a surprise. I want it to be a story you can tell forever. I also don't want these two idiots to be a part of it."

Harper barked out a laugh, genuinely amused. "It's okay. We have plenty of time. I want to focus on the move and Christmas, too. I swear I'm not upset about this."

"Good." Jared was relieved. "I'm glad."

"These two are going to keep torturing you now that they know they can, though." Harper's smile was rueful. "Sorry."

"We're definitely going to torture you," Zander agreed.

"Yeah." Jason bobbed his head. "I'm mostly excited that I still have a shot, though. That's the thing I want to focus on."

"You don't still have a shot," Jared snapped. "Not even a little shot."

"We'll see."

"Ugh."

Harper chuckled as she squeezed Jared's knee under the table. "You were going to tell us something about Colin Thompson before we got distracted. How about you focus on that?"

"Yeah," Zander agreed, turning serious. "He's not our murderer, is he?"

"No." Jared turned somber. "He did have a very interesting story about Maggie trying to arrange a bank heist, though."

Now it was Harper's turn to be flabbergasted. "What?"

"Yeah. It seems we have a break in our case. Sit back with your pumpkin delight and I'll tell you all about it."

## 16

# SIXTEEN

J ared remained slightly unnerved throughout lunch and he was lost in his own head as he helped Harper into her hoodie when they were ready to leave.

"Are you in there?" Harper snapped her fingers in Jared's face to get his attention, causing him to jolt.

Jared forced his eyes to Harper's placid features. "What? Did you say something, Heart?"

Harper offered him a lopsided grin. "Where were you just now?"

"I was ... thinking about you." That wasn't a lie, Jared rationalized. He really had been thinking about her. "You're not upset, are you?"

Harper's eyebrows hopped. "Upset about what?"

"All of it. Everything Jason and Zander said. I mean ... do we need to talk about this further?"

"Oh, *that*." Harper relaxed a bit. "I'm not upset about that. "You don't need to worry about that."

She was so easygoing Jared had trouble believing she was telling the truth. "But it would be normal for you to be upset about that."

"Maybe I'm not normal."

"You're definitely not normal," Jared agreed. "That doesn't mean you don't have feelings and I want to make sure we're okay."

Harper's smile was so sunny and serene it was impossible for Jared not to return it.

"I'm fine, Jared. You're the one who let them work you up. There's no reason for it. I'm excited about how things are now and I'm looking forward to what comes in the future. I'm a big proponent of believing that things work out how they're supposed to work out."

Jared wasn't sure he believed it was that easy when feelings and emotions were involved, but he decided to let it pass ... for now. "I just want us to be okay." He leaned forward and graced her with a soft kiss on the corner of her mouth. "What do you plan on doing with the rest of your day?"

"Oh, that was a sneaky way to switch things around," Harper teased. "As for the rest of the day, I thought Zander and I would make a stop at the Standish barn and help Ezra pass over. Then I thought we would play it by ear."

Jared wasn't thrilled with the news. "Do you have to go to the barn? I mean, as far as we know that's the last place Maggie was seen alive. It might not be safe."

Harper snorted. "I'm fairly certain I know how to take care of myself. You don't have to worry about that. As for the barn being safe, I don't think that's a concern. If Maggie was taken from there, it was at night and she was lured during a party. I won't have either of those things working against me today."

Jared brightened considerably. "Good point. I still want you to be safe."

"I have every intention of being safe." Harper meant it. "What are you going to do with your afternoon?"

"I want to talk to this Jay Forrester," Jared replied without hesitation. "If he really was plotting with Maggie, he might be the one who killed her to cover up that fact."

Harper tilted her head to the side, considering. "I get that. At least I kind of get that. If they hadn't carried out the plan, though, why would Jay need to kill her? I can see killing her to cover his tracks if they really managed to pull it off. I can't see killing her before they ever stole anything."

Jared hated to admit it, but Harper had a point. "We still have to talk to him. This is the first really solid lead that we've gotten. I don't have all the answers yet."

"Then talk to him." Harper rolled to the balls of her feet and gave Jared a firm kiss. "Let me know if you find out anything. I'm as eager to put this one behind us as you are."

Jared wasn't sure that was true. "I'll call you when I know more. You do the same if you get in trouble at the barn. In fact, text me when you get there and when you're leaving so I don't worry."

"Yes, sir." Harper offered up a saucy wink as she mock-saluted and grinned.

"Very cute." Jared ran his hand down Harper's arm and smiled. "I'll be in touch."

"I'm looking forward to you being in touch."

Jared couldn't help but smile. She was too bubbly and adorable not to grin. "I love you."

Harper sobered. "I love you, too. Don't worry about the other stuff. It's going to work itself out. I promise."

"I'm not worried." That wasn't completely true. "I'll be in touch."

"I'll be waiting."


**JARED AND MEL TRACKED** down Jay Forrester at his father's car dealership. The kid was out to lunch, but the father – Joe Forrester – happened to be in his office and was more than willing to entertain two police officers until his offspring returned.

"Cripes. What did Jay do now?" Joe seemed resigned as he took his seat at his desk.

"We want to talk to him about his relationship with Maggie Harris," Mel supplied, causing Joe to furrow his brow.

"Why does that name sound familiar to me? I swear I've heard that name ... and recently."

"She's the woman we found in the Whisper Cove Cemetery the other night," Jared replied, his voice even. "We understand she had ties to your son and we want to sort out exactly what those ties were."

Joe's mouth dropped open as realization washed over him. "You can't be serious. You think Jay killed that girl? My understanding is that you had no leads on that. At least that's what they're saying at the coffee shop."

"Well, if you heard it at the coffee shop," Mel drawled, shifting on his chair.

"You know what I mean." Joe refused to back down. "Everyone says there's no motivation for killing that girl – that she wasn't raped or anything – so it's a big mystery. I can't understand how that leads you to questioning Jay."

"We've been following some leads." Mel chose his words carefully. "One of those leads directed us toward some kids Maggie was spending her time with. It seems she was going to Dave & Buster's twice a week and meeting with this one particular group, which happened to include your son."

Joe almost looked relieved at the explanation. "Oh, so you're talking to everyone in that group, right?"

"We've talked to at least one other member at this time," Jared hedged. "He's the one who told us a rather interesting story about Jay."

"Story?" Joe pursed his lips. "I'm almost afraid to ask. I'm sure Jay has quite a few stories to tell these days."

"I'm sure he does, too. I'm specifically talking about the story where he let himself into your safe and grabbed cash to spend at the bar."

"Oh." Joe exhaled heavily, his face twisting. "I guess I should've known it was impossible for that story to stay secret."

"One of the kids who was hanging around Jay said that he was acting like a big shot at Dave & Buster's," Mel offered helpfully. "He was essentially flashing a big wad of cash for a time and that's how he lured Maggie."

"She was only interested in people with money," Jared added. "She thought Jay had money until the truth came out and she realized he didn't have funds of his own and was merely letting you bankroll his extravagances. I believe that caused some strife."

"I didn't know Maggie other than to wave when I was at the bank." Joe stroked his chin as he considered the predicament. "She seemed nice enough, but I didn't know her. I certainly didn't know she was messing around with Jay."

"What did you know?" Mel asked.

Joe held his hands out and shrugged. "I knew that money came up missing from my safe and that I couldn't figure out how ... at least at first. It never even occurred to me that it was Jay. I guess you probably find that naïve ... but I didn't even consider him."

"I don't think most parents would immediately jump to the conclusion that their kid was ripping them off." Mel was sympathetic to Joe's plight. He understood why the man was so upset ... and reticent. "You must have uncovered the truth at some point, though."

Joe bobbed his head. "I did. I set up a camera. I assumed I would catch a secretary or one of my other salesmen breaking into the safe. I wasn't sure how anyone was getting into my private office, but I figured the camera would show me how and I could plug that hole after the fact. I got an eyeful of something else."

"What did you do when you realized what was going on?" Jared asked.

"I confronted Jay. At first, he denied it – acted all wounded and everything that I would dare consider him – and then I showed him the camera. He had the gall to threaten to sue me for filming him without his knowledge. It was ... so ridiculous."

"You could've turned him in to the police," Mel pointed out. "He was stealing from you. You were well within your rights to have him carted off. It might've taught him a lesson."

"It might have," Joe agreed. "I was actually going to do that, wipe my hands of him. Then his mother got involved. Things haven't been great between us for the past two years – we've even talked about divorce – but she was so broken-hearted I couldn't send the kid to prison no matter how angry I was.

"We came to a meeting of the minds instead," he continued. "She agreed to go to counseling with me to try to save the marriage and I agreed not to press charges against Jay. I even kept him at the dealership, although I took away his keys and changed the combination on the safe. He's strictly an employee now. He no longer gets perks for being the boss's son."

"How has that been working out?"

Joe shrugged. "It's a work in progress. I would be lying if I said there were times I didn't want to pop that kid's head like a zit. He's my son, though. I'm trying to get past it."

"Well, I don't think what's about to happen is going to help that zit thing." Mel's smile was rueful. "In fact ... ." He didn't get a chance to finish because Joe's office door swung open to reveal a sullen-looking young man in an ill-fitting gray suit.

"I'm back from lunch, Dad," the man drawled. "As per your request that I check in with you before doing anything ... I'm going to walk the lot now and see if I can find someone looking to buy a car."

"Thank you for your succinct report, Jay," Joe drawled, his eyes firing with animosity as he glared at his only son. "I also want to thank you for not knocking."

Jay rolled his eyes. "I don't remember you instructing me to knock."

"It's simple courtesy."

"Oh, well, I'll do better next time." Jay didn't back down, instead shaking his head as he muttered something under his breath that no one could make out. "Can I go now?"

"No." Joe immediately started shaking his head. "I need you to come in here and talk to these fine police officers from Whisper Cove. They're here to see you, not me."

Jared didn't miss the way Jay's demeanor shifted, the young man's eyes turning furtive as his shoulders slouched.

"Come sit over here, Jay," Mel instructed, gesturing toward a third chair at the edge of the room. "We have some questions for you."

"What kind of questions?" Jay remained rooted to his spot, as if he were close to panicking.

"Well, why don't you wait until they ask them and go from there?" Joe suggested, frowning. "Sit down, Jay."

The young man made a face as he scuffed his shoes against the linoleum and took his seat next to Mel. It was obvious Jay was furious at the turn of events, but he was in no position to start demanding answers so he merely sat and placed his hands on his knees.

Jared inclined his chin to prod Mel into asking the first question.

"So, Jay, we understand you had a relationship of sorts with Maggie Harris," Mel started.

Jay immediately balked. "We didn't have a relationship. We knew each other to say 'hi.' That was it."

"So, you didn't entice her with your father's money and then get forced to own up to the fact that you were broke?"

Jay's eyes widened to comical proportions. "No ... yes ... I ... who told you that?" Jay's eyes narrowed to glittery slits.

"It doesn't matter who told us that," Jared replied, drawing Jay's attention. "We want to hear your side of it."

"I don't have a side." Jay folded his arms across his chest. "I mean ... I really don't have a side of it. I barely knew Maggie."

"And yet the two of you were making plans to rob the bank together," Mel noted, biting the inside of his cheek to keep from laughing at the way the color drained from Jay's features. "My understanding is that it was still in the talking phase, but I'm sure you can understand that we have a few questions."

"Oh, for the love of ... ." Joe slapped his hand to his forehead, dumbfounded.

"I was not going to rob the bank!" Jay turned so shrill he almost sounded like a panicking teenage girl. "Whoever told you that is crazy ... and dead."

Jared and Mel exchanged a weighted look, something unsaid passing between them.

"I'm going to tell you how I think it went down," Jared said after a beat, leaning forward and positioning himself so Jay had no choice but to look into his eyes. "You tell me if I'm wrong and we'll go from there."

"I was not planning on stealing from the bank," Jay screeched. "You were wrong about that."

Jared held up his hand to quiet Jay. "You were pretending to be a big man with the group at Dave & Buster's. You had money and that made you popular. You bought a lot of drinks and food and your friends basically worshipped you because of it.

"Then your father caught you in the act of stealing and overnight all of your funds dried up," he continued. "You were still hanging with the same group of friends, but you were no longer the big hero. You were just one of the gang, and you didn't like that.

"On top of everything else, Maggie started losing interest when she realized you didn't have money because that's all she cared about," Jared said. "You realized, if you wanted to keep her close, you were going to have to come up with money. That's why you suggested the bank robbery."

Jay made a squeaking sound.

Jared barreled forward, ignoring the pathetic noise. "I don't think you really intended to rob the bank. Honestly, you don't have the stones. Maggie was intrigued enough to plot, though, and that meant she continued hanging around ... which is all you really cared about."

"I was not going to rob the bank!" Jay was firm. "Do I look like an idiot?"

Mel and Jared exchanged another look, causing Joe to sigh.

"That's a loaded question, son," Joe snapped. "I think, from their perspective, you look like a massive idiot. I'm hopeful they're right and you were just talking big, though. If not, you're dumber than I thought and I just know I'm going to break your mother's heart when I tell her this one."

Jay made an exaggerated face as he worked his jaw. "I don't know what you want me to say," he said finally. "I am not going to admit to plotting to rob the bank."

Mel bobbed his head in understanding. "Well, that's probably the smartest thing you've said or done in weeks."

"Robbing the bank was just something you talked about to pass the time, right?" Jared prodded. "You didn't have a real plan, did you?"

Jay held his hands palms out and shrugged. "I didn't have a plan. I just wanted to keep spending time with Maggie. She was pretty."

"That's what I figured."

"That doesn't mean Maggie didn't have a plan with someone else," Jay added, taking Mel and Jared by surprise with the offhand comment. "She was fickle and went after whoever could offer her the best way to get her hands on that money. That's why I'm not even a little bit sorry that she's dead."

Joe made a disgusted sound in the back of his throat. "Watch your mouth, boy. That's no way to speak of the dead."

"It's not my fault that she was a whore who would go after anyone who had a plan to actually rob the bank," Jay snapped. "I didn't make her that way."

Jared straightened in his chair. "And who are you talking about?"

"Danny Wood." Jay wasn't reluctant in the least to turn over on someone he formerly considered a friend. "He and Maggie were plotting a way to get their hands on the vault key, and according to him, Maggie was extremely close to accomplishing it. Then she turned up dead and Danny stopped coming around. I don't think that's a coincidence."

"Huh." Mel rubbed the back of his neck as he considered the statement. "I guess we're going to need to hear the rest of that story."

Jay realized too late what he'd blurted out. "Oh, man. This is going to come back to bite me, isn't it?"

"Not as much as it could have under different circumstances," Jared replied. "You need to talk, though. We need to hear the rest of it."

"Fine. I'm doing this under duress, though."

"Duly noted."

## SEVENTEEN

Harper and Zander stopped by the office long enough to gather supplies for their trip to the barn. Even though they paid for the space, in truth, they didn't spend a lot of time at the office. It had become Eric and Molly's domain and that was clearly on display upon entering the storefront location and finding the younger half of the GHI team cuddling on the couch.

"Oh, I'm going to throw up," Zander complained as he slapped his hand over his eyes. "Someone point me toward the bathroom. I think I'm blind."

Harper ignored Zander's theatrics and pressed her lips together as Eric and Molly scrambled to detach from one another. She didn't miss the fact that Molly's shirt appeared to be untucked and askew. "Um ... hey, guys."

Eric recovered first. "Hi. I ... did we know you guys were coming?" His face was unbelievably red as he smoothed Molly's shirt and did his best to appear professional. "We were just taking a break, by the way. This is not how we've been spending our afternoons while you guys have been busy with tours."

"Not at all," Molly added, hurriedly combing her fingers through her short hair. "We treat this place like a business and are always professional. I ... we were simply on a break."

"Uh-huh." It took everything Harper had to refrain from laughing. "Next time you guys are on a break, you might want to lock the front door. We have a sign that says when we'll be back from a break and everything."

"Right." Eric looked as if he wanted to find a hole to crawl into and disappear. "I'll definitely try to remember that next time we're on a break."

"Which won't be until tomorrow," Molly added, her cheeks flushed with color. "We only take one break a day for lunch."

"Then you should definitely lock the door," Zander encouraged. "That way you would hear us fiddling with the lock when we enter and you'll have time to arrange your clothes and pretend you weren't groping each other on the office couch."

Molly's forced smile slipped. "We weren't groping."

Harper helpfully leaned forward and adjusted Molly's top so her brightly-colored bra wasn't on display. "Just lock the door next time." She cleared her throat and ignored Molly's mortification as she straightened. "Other than taking a break, do you guys have anything going on today?"

"We have a few things," Eric muttered as he pushed himself to a standing position and ran a hand through his hair. He met Zander's amused gaze with a hard one of his own. "I know what you're thinking and I don't care. We weren't doing anything."

Zander held up his hands in a placating manner. "I didn't say you were doing anything. In fact, I think what you were not doing was kind of cute ... although also traumatic for me because Molly looks like a little kid sometimes."

"I am not a little kid," Molly snapped, her fiery temper on full display. "Don't say things like that to him because then he'll start thinking about it and it will turn into a whole big thing. I'm an adult. I can drink and everything."

Last time Harper checked Molly could barely drink, but she decided to let it go. "You said you had a few things to work on. What are they?"

"Research," Eric answered, shuffling to his desk and taking the chair behind it so he could focus on his computer. "The people from that old theater in Mount Clemens called because they think they have a ghost. They don't want to pay for our full line of services until they decide how likely it is that they have a bad haunting, though, so I'm doing a run on the building and sending it to them."

"Oh." Harper was intrigued. "I've always wanted to see inside that building. I get a feeling that someone is watching me whenever I pass. It's been empty for years, though. Did someone just buy it?"

Eric nodded. "Yeah. Some guy is going to turn it into a club or something. He's got workers in there now but swears people keep hearing whispering. Oh, and a few things have fallen over. The workers think it's a ghost, he's irritated, and I'm doing research to see what I can find."

"Anything?"

Eric shrugged. "Two unexplained deaths in the seventies. One disappearance in the eighties. I'm still drilling down. I'll email you a report when I have it."

"That sounds good." Harper moved to her desk, frowning when she saw the stack of files waiting for her. "What's all this?"

"That's the normal Halloween calls we've received," Molly replied. "Everyone sees ghosts this time of year and they want us to do something about it. They almost always turn out to be nothing, but you usually want to look at the call stubs all the same."

"I almost forgot about that." Harper was thoughtful as she sat at her desk, flicking a gaze to Zander and Eric as they started talking about something else and moving to the storefront's back room where GHI's equipment was kept. "Things look to be going well between you and Eric."

Molly risked a glance over her shoulder, relief evident when she realized the men had disappeared. "Things are going really well and I'm not sure what to do." Molly was enthusiastic by nature, but Harper couldn't resist the way the young woman's eyes sparkled as she perched on the corner of Harper's desk. "I need your advice."

"You need my advice? About Eric?" Harper was understandably surprised. Eric spent almost two years crushing on her before settling into a relationship with Molly. During that time, Molly crushed on Eric to the point where it was almost painful. It took Eric forever to see what was right in front of him because he was too focused on Harper to look. The knowledge left Harper feeling uncomfortable at the oddest of times. "I'm not sure I'm the right person to give you advice on Eric."

Molly made an exaggerated face. "Wow. You're kind of a trip when you want to be, huh? I'm not asking you for advice on Eric. Er, well, I'm not directly asking you for advice on Eric. It's more that I want advice on maintaining a healthy relationship in general."

"Oh." Harper wasn't expecting that. "Okay, um ... I guess I can try to help. How come you want advice from me, though? I don't think I'm exactly what anyone would call an expert."

"No, but you have a healthy relationship with Jared. I mean ... you guys are moving in together and everything. You're the only person I know who has a healthy relationship going on right now so you're like a unicorn in my book."

No matter how worldly she liked to consider herself, Harper liked the idea of being equated to a unicorn. "Okay, shoot. I'll do my best to answer questions."

"Great." Molly rubbed her hands together as she checked to make sure they were still alone. "How do you get a man to put the toilet seat down when he's finished doing his business? I don't want to be a nag, but there's nothing more annoying than a splashdown in the middle of the night."

The question was the exact opposite of what Harper expected. That didn't mean she was bereft of suggestions. "Take a seat. I could write a manifesto on that one."

"Yay!" Molly clapped her hands. "I knew you wouldn't let me down."

"Oh, men are tricky beasts. You have to tame them but not let them know they're being tamed. You might want to grab a notebook and pen. I have a lot of wisdom to share."

"I'm on it."

**"THIS PLACE IS AN** absolute dump."

Jared made a face and kept his hands close to his body so he wouldn't inadvertently touch something as he stood in front of a ramshackle apartment door.

"It is a dump," Mel agreed. "I can't believe this place is up to code. I mean ... there's a hole in the floor over there." He pointed for emphasis. "I can't believe the New Haven building inspectors haven't shut this place down."

"Maybe they have more on their minds."

"Maybe. Let's see if Danny is here and then make a break for it," Mel suggested. "I don't want to be here longer than I have to."

"That sounds like a plan." Jared rapped on the thin door three times in rapid succession, adopting a professional if somewhat detached demeanor when Danny opened the door and glared between faces. "Mr. Wood?"

For his part, Danny looked as if the last thing he wanted was to entertain guests. "Whatever you're selling, I'm not interested in buying." He moved to shut the door, but Jared slid his foot between the door and jamb to stop him. "Do you want to get your ass kicked?"

Jared ignored the man's tone. He figured it was mostly bravado, an act of sorts, but he wasn't afraid to throw down if need be. "My name is Jared Monroe. I'm a detective with the Whisper Cove Police Department. This is my partner Mel Kelsey. We have some questions for you."

Danny didn't immediately respond other than blinking ... and sneering. Slowly he began to collect himself, though, and the look he shot Jared was right out of a bad eighties movie where rival gangs were about to fight. "And what if I don't want to answer questions?"

"Then we'll have to take you into custody and transport you to the police department," Mel answered without hesitation. "It's up to you."

Danny worked his jaw, belligerence evident, but ultimately he pushed open the door. "Come on in." The false bravado was back. "I would offer you a refreshment, but I'm out."

"I can see that," Jared muttered in disgust as he stepped over discarded beer bottles and followed the man into what could loosely be described as a living room. "We don't want to take up much of your time, but we need some information."

"About what?"

"Maggie Harris."

Danny either couldn't or wouldn't hide his shock. "Maggie? The hot chick who worked at the bank?"

Jared nodded, refusing to sit even as Danny threw himself onto a filthy couch and motioned to the chairs across the way. "I'm fine standing. Thank you, though."

If Danny recognized why Jared didn't want to sit, he didn't show it. "I don't understand why you want to talk about Maggie. I barely knew her."

"But you are aware that she was found at the cemetery the other night, right?" Mel queried. "You know she was murdered."

Danny's eyebrows hopped. "I knew she was dead. I didn't know she was murdered. The newspaper and television just said she was found under suspicious circumstances. I thought that could mean anything."

"I guess that's fair." Mel made a face as he considered sitting in one of the chairs but ultimately opted to remain standing. He was genuinely afraid some critter might be crawling around in the fabric and he didn't want to take bedbugs home if he could help it. "We need to know about your relationship with Maggie."

"And what makes you think I had a relationship with Maggie?"

"We've heard from several people that you were spending time together," Jared replied. "I'm going to guess that time didn't involve visits here."

"And why do you assume that?" Danny was doing his best to appear courageous and nonchalant, but Jared could read the tenseness settling over the man's shoulders.

"Because Maggie was all about money and this place doesn't lend itself to pretending you have money," Jared replied honestly. "She wanted a rich guy and you're very clearly not rich."

Danny barked out a hollow laugh. "No, I'm not rich. That doesn't mean I don't do well with the ladies. Most women want a bad boy they think they can mold. I let them think I'm that bad boy and I do quite well."

"That wasn't what Maggie was after, though," Mel pointed out. "Maggie wanted financial stability. It was more important to her than street cred or looks. The money was her driving force."

Danny held his hands palms out and shrugged. "You guys seem to know a lot about Maggie and what she did and didn't want. If you know so much, why are you here? I don't have anything to offer you as far as Maggie is concerned."

"I think that's partially true," Jared countered. "I think you can offer us one thing, though."

"And what's that?"

"Your plan to steal from the bank."

For one brief moment, Danny looked like a deer caught in headlights. He continued to blink, but his breath lodged in his throat and he sputtered until he regained control of himself. "What? I don't know what you're talking about."

"Oh, don't bother playing that game," Jared chided, his discomfort at being trapped in the filthy apartment continuously growing. "We know you tried to lure Maggie in by telling her you had a plan to rob the bank. She was looking for a way to make money – mostly because her efforts at snagging a man who she thought had money and would fund the lifestyle she wanted were falling short – and this was the idea she came up with."

"She talked about it with Jay Forrester first," Mel added. "She realized pretty quickly that he was all talk when it came to an actual plan, though. That's when she turned to you."

Danny narrowed his eyes. "Is Jay the one who told you all this?"

"We have multiple sources," Mel lied. He saw no reason to point the finger at Jay when the kid had so many other problems. Besides, his father was going to handle the punishment for Jay this go around and Mel had a feeling it was going to be a dark reckoning. There was no reason to add to the mayhem. "What we want to know is how far you made it with the plan."

Danny touched his tongue to his lip as he internally debated how to answer. "I think maybe I should shut this down and get a lawyer."

"And I think you didn't make it far when it came to planning and you were all talk, just like Jay," Mel shot back. "We need to know, though. Maggie is dead. She was murdered. If this has something to do with your plan, we need to know about it."

Danny exhaled heavily as he ran his hand through his hair. He looked defeated. "I don't know what to tell you. We talked about it. You already know that. It wasn't so much a plan as a bunch of boasting, though. There was no way we had anything actionable."

Mel pursed his lips. "That's what I figured. We still need to know the basics, though."

"The basics?" Danny held out his hands. "The basics were simple. If we wanted to steal from the bank we needed a vault key. That would have to fall to Maggie since the rest of us didn't have access to anyone with a key.

"She said she was going to seduce the bank manager and steal his key," he continued. "To my knowledge, she was still trying to worm her way into his good graces. The plan was to have sex with him enough times that he trusted her. Once she got that far into things, then we would pick a day and wait until she could get him alone.

"Then she planned to drug him and steal his key," he continued. "Once she had the key we were going to load up her car with stuff, break into the bank vault, and steal as much cash as we could carry before making a break for it."

"And that's it?" Jared asked. "You didn't get any further than that?"

"No. It was just big talk for something that was never going to happen. I mean ... basically we talked about robbing the bank because it was fun to dream about how life would be if we could afford to buy anything we wanted. She didn't even implement the first part of the plan, though, unless you call flirting with that schlub who runs the bank as implementation."

Mel tilted his head to the side as he flicked a gaze to Jared. "Mark didn't mention Maggie flirting when we talked to him."

"He didn't," Jared agreed. "He might not have recognized it as flirting."

"Oh, Maggie wasn't subtle," Danny interjected. "If she wanted to flirt, there's no way he could mistake it for something else. She was really obvious."

Mel traced his thumb over his bottom lip. "I guess we could go

LILY HARPER HART

back and talk to Mark. He's a pain in the butt most of the time, but he's usually pretty forthcoming. If he didn't mention Maggie flirting with him, there might be a reason."

Jared nodded. He was eager to get out of the apartment, even if it meant returning to the bank. "I think that's probably the best way to go."

"Great," Danny enthused. "Does that mean I'm off the hook?"

"It means you probably shouldn't leave the state," Mel clarified. "We might not be done with you."

"Oh, now why would I want to leave all this?" Danny drawled. "That's just crazy talk."

Even though he found the young man's attitude lacking, Jared couldn't help the wave of sympathy from washing over him. "I hope things start looking up for you."

"Yeah, that would be nice. I won't hold my breath, though."

# EIGHTEEN

"That is fascinating stuff." Molly was rapt as Harper laid out the rules of spending a boatload of time with men. "So you're saying that you can't tell a man what to do. You have to lead him to the water and let him think it's his idea to drink, so to speak."

Harper bobbed her head. "That's exactly what I'm saying."

"Wow. I never would've thought to do it that way." Molly tapped her painted fingernails on the desktop, thoughtful. "That's genius. How did you come up with that?"

Harper was amused. "I grew up with a best friend who also happened to be a man. To be fair, his mother told me how to get him to do stuff, though, so I'm hardly the one who came up with this plan of action."

"Still, it's genius."

"It's a load of a crap is what it is," Zander announced, strolling into the room with Eric on his heels. He had a handheld EMF reader in his hand and a scowl on his face. "I can't believe you just filled her head with all that nonsense, Harp. I'm really disappointed in you."

Harper refused to be ashamed despite being caught. "I stand by what I said."

"And how did this lovely conversation start?" Eric asked, his eyes on Molly as he sat at his desk. His expression was hard to read but he didn't look particularly upset. "I mean ... how did a subject like this even pop up?"

"Oh, well ... ." Harper shifted on her chair, unwilling to throw Molly under the bus.

"I asked about building a strong relationship," Molly replied without hesitation. "This is my first real relationship and I wanted to make sure that I didn't do something stupid to alienate you."

Eric was taken aback. "I see. Um ... why is it you think you're going to alienate me?"

Molly shrugged, noncommittal. "Because we're still in the honeymoon phase of our relationship. We're still at that point where I find everything you do cute and entertaining and you find everything I do endearing and adorable."

Eric leaned back in his chair. "At the risk of starting a fight I don't want to finish, what makes you think that I find everything you do endearing and adorable?"

Now it was Molly's turn to be caught off guard. "Why wouldn't you find everything I do amazing and entertaining?"

"Well, for starters, it's impossible for one person to be perfectly adorable twenty-four hours a day." Eric chose his words carefully. "I find you adorable a good eighteen hours out of every day. The other six hours are more of a struggle."

Molly's mouth dropped open. "Excuse me?"

Eric refused to back down. "You heard me. You're not perfect. I'm not perfect either. I would much rather you just tell me when something is bothering you than do that thing Harper was talking about. I prefer honesty and think it's a two-way road. If I'm doing something irritating, I want you to tell me. If you do something irritating, I'll do the same."

Molly balked. "I'm not sure I want to know that you find parts of my personality irritating. Isn't that a surefire trip to fightland?"

"Couples fight." Eric was matter-of-fact. "That's what they do. The key is to move past those fights with a stronger relationship. I thought we were both on the same page there."

"We are." Molly chewed on her bottom lip before turning back to Harper. "Do you and Jared fight?"

Harper nodded. "We do. It's usually nothing major, but we definitely fight. I don't think you can have a real relationship without fighting."

"Just this afternoon they fought over why Jared doesn't want to marry her," Zander offered helpfully. "I was there and it was ugly."

Harper made a face. "We did not fight about that."

"You did so."

"We did not!"

"Not that I want to get in the middle of this because I'm worried it's going to turn into war, but why aren't you guys getting married?" Eric asked, raising his hands to quiet Harper and Zander before they got full heads of steam and tipped the conversation in a direction no one wanted to follow. "I would think the normal thing to do was get engaged and *then* move in together. Is there a reason you're not doing things that way?"

"Yes." Zander was somber. "It's that whole cow and getting the milk for free thing. I'm afraid Harper has fallen prey to it."

"That did it." Harper moved to get to her feet, but Molly wisely shoved her boss back down before Harper could gain her balance.

"Let's not fight," Molly suggested. "There's no reason to fight over this. If Jared hasn't proposed yet, he must have a good reason."

"He does," Harper agreed. "The house across the way opened up and it was absolutely perfect for our needs. We couldn't risk letting it go. We might be doing things a little backward, but that doesn't mean we'll end up in a bad spot.

"That house is absolutely perfect for us and there's only one house that fits the bill," she continued. "We need the house. Now we have the house. The other stuff will happen when it's supposed to happen."

"And you really believe that?" Molly couldn't help being impressed. "You really believe things happen because they're supposed to happen, don't you?"

"I deal with ghosts and death on a regular basis," Harper replied. "I think I have to believe in a world order or I would go crazy. As for

Jared and me, I'm happy. I don't remember ever being this happy before. Why wouldn't that be enough for me?"

Molly shrugged. "I don't know. I guess I'm just curious why Jared didn't propose."

"Oh, I wouldn't worry about that," Zander said, chuckling. "I honestly think the thought never crossed his mind because he was too focused on the house. Now that it's been brought up, though, I'm pretty sure that's all he's going to be thinking about."

Harper's mouth dropped open. "That's what you wanted all along, isn't it? You wanted someone to ask Jared why he didn't propose. You would've done it yourself, but you knew he would ignore the question if it came from you."

Zander adopted an innocent expression. "I have no idea what you mean. I thought you wanted to go out to the barn to put Ezra Standish to bed before dark. Wasn't that the plan? Isn't that why we stopped here for equipment?"

"Oh, don't do that." Harper made an admonishing sound in the back of her throat as she wagged her finger. "I know exactly what you're doing and I don't like it. At all. I mean ... even a little."

"That's rich coming from you given how you were instructing Molly to manipulate Eric to get what she wants."

"That's different," Harper protested. "That was about training him to put the toilet seat down – which is something all men should automatically do, by the way – and not about trying to trick a man into proposing when he's not ready."

"Who said anything about tricking him?" Zander was affronted. "I want him to be fully cognizant of his actions when he does it. Oh, and mark my words, Harp, he's going to do it a lot sooner now because it's in his brain and he won't be able to shake it."

Harper openly gaped. "You think he's going to propose?"

"I think Christmas and Valentine's Day are right around the corner and Jason opened his big, fat mouth at the exact right time. Sure, Jason asked for different reasons than me – he's hopeful he still has a shot – but the outcome was the same. You're going to end up with a husband out of this. You're welcome."

It took everything Harper had not to launch herself across the desk so she could wrap her hands around Zander's neck. "We should probably be going." She was terse, her tone cold. "We have things to do."

"That's what I said five minutes ago."

"While we're doing those things, we're going to have a really long talk."

Zander heaved out a sigh. "Fine. If we're going to talk, though, we're going to put multiple things on the table. I want to talk about the color pink for your kitchen, for example. If we're going to talk, we're going to talk about all of it."

"Fine," Harper gritted out.

"Great." Zander brightened considerably. "Do you want to stop for pumpkin lattes on the way?"

"Of course. We're not animals."


**MARK CROWLEY WAS OBVIOUSLY** caught off guard when he showed Jared and Mel into his office. He wasn't expecting an interruption – in fact had strictly forbidden his secretary from bothering him – and was mildly agitated (to say the least) when she timidly knocked on his door. After explaining exactly who was there, though, Mark had no choice but to allow the two men into his office.

"This is a nice surprise," Mark drawled. "I can't remember the last time I got to spend more than five minutes in the same week with members of Whisper Cove's finest."

"Cut the crap, Mark," Mel chided. "We don't need you to blow sunshine up our behinds. We're well aware you're not happy to see us."

"Whew!" Mark mockingly swiped at his brow. "I'm glad that's out in the open." He rolled his eyes as he sat. "What are you guys doing here? I assume it has something to do with Maggie, although for the life of me I can't figure out what because I've told you everything I know."

"And we believed you at the time," Jared supplied. "Unfortunately for you, a few things have come up over the course of our investigation and now we have more questions."

"And what might those questions be?"

"For starters, did you have a romantic relationship with Maggie?"

Whatever he was expecting, that wasn't it. Mark was either genuinely flabbergasted or one of the best actors Jared had ever crossed paths with.

"Did you just ask if I was ... you know, doing stuff ... with Maggie?" Mark swallowed hard. "I can't believe you actually asked me that."

"Well, believe it." Mel was firm. "The girl had a certain reputation and you came up in regard to her plans for this bank so we have to ask."

Mark wrinkled his brow. "I don't know what that means."

"Then let us break it down for you," Jared suggested. "Maggie was after money. She didn't care who she had to date to get it."

"I believe I'm the one who told you that."

"Not the only one. A lot of other people told us the same. She was jumping from man to man in an effort to find someone to fund a life-style she could enjoy. She didn't care about looks or pedigree. She only cared about money, and that includes going after married men."

"I'm a married man," Mark reminded them. "I have a wife and two children. How can you possibly think that I would have a relationship with Maggie? The entire thing is ... ludicrous."

There was something about the way Mark reacted to the accusation that set Jared's teeth on edge. He couldn't decide if he believed the man – and he was leaning toward a resounding "no" on that front – but there was nothing to indicate he was lying either. Everything felt more unsettled than nefarious.

"Ludicrous, huh?" Jared exchanged a quick look with Mel. "What would you say if I told you that Maggie was openly plotting with several younger men to find a way into the bank vault?"

"What?"

Jared nodded. "She was. She talked to at least two people we've questioned and she was trying to come up with a way to break into the vault so she could steal. One of those plans included seducing you."

Mark's face turned red as he fidgeted with his tie, loosening it so he could breathe. "That is ridiculous. I would say I don't believe you."

"It's true, though," Mel said. "Maggie was openly talking with two guys and trying to get them to help her steal from the bank. I don't believe she stumbled across a plan that would work, but that doesn't mean she wasn't going to give it the old college try.

"The thing is, the second plan involved you in a way that makes me curious whether she at least tried to implement it," he continued. "The plan was to seduce you, make you trust her, then drug you one night after sex. Once that task was complete, she was going to steal the vault key and take her accomplice to the location so they could load up."

Mark grew redder. "But that makes no sense. It never would've worked. She would need more than the key to put that plan into action."

"Oh, don't get me wrong, I don't think the plan would've worked," Mel noted. "I don't think Maggie was smart enough to make it work. I think she had a dream she couldn't see past. That dream was being rich and buying whatever she wanted without having to work for it. That doesn't mean she wasn't plotting."

"But ... no." Mark vehemently shook his head. "She would need more than the vault key. You need two vault keys. Two people have to put their keys in at the same time to get it to open. The system was designed that way."

"Okay, so who else has vault keys?"

"Five people here have keys. Other than me, three of them are women. I don't see how Maggie thought she would be able to get her hands on two keys."

"Did everyone here know you needed two keys?"

"Well ... ." Mark broke off as he tilted his head to the side. "I don't know. The vault is on the basement floor and the tellers aren't allowed to go down there. We usually have the day's money upstairs and divided into boxes by the time the tellers arrive. Those boxes are kept in a separate, much smaller vault." He appeared lost in thought. "You only need one key to open that vault. Not much money is kept there, though."

"Maggie might not have realized that," Jared said. "She might have thought you kept everything in the smaller vault. I'm starting to get the feeling she wasn't the sharpest key on the ring."

"I guess." Mark scratched his chin. "Who was she working with to accomplish this?"

"Two men who didn't really want to rob the bank," Mel replied. "They basically enjoyed flirting with Maggie – maybe more, who knows – and they put up with her bank robbing tall tales to keep the relationships going. I don't get the feeling that either of them were actually willing to risk robbing the bank."

"So, what does that have to do with Maggie's murder?"

"We don't know." Jared opted for telling the truth. "It could have nothing to do with it. The thing is, I can tell something is up with you. I don't know what that something is, but you're very obviously hiding something from us. We can't help unless you tell us."

"Is that true, Mark?" Mel prodded. "Are you hiding something from us?"

"I'm hiding something ... different," Mark replied, resigned. "It's not that I was hiding something from you as much as I simply didn't want anyone to know. It puts my marriage at risk."

"You slept with Maggie, didn't you?" Jared made a tsking sound and shook his head. "You let her seduce you and now you feel like an idiot because of it."

"I didn't let her seduce me," Mark shot back. "I don't like that word, by the way. It's a stupid word and makes me sound weak when I wasn't weak."

"So how would you describe it?"

"It's not what you think." Mark was adamant. "Also, I didn't have sex with Maggie. I know you think I did, but I didn't. I'm not that stupid."

Jared scratched at an invisible itch on the side of his nose, legitimately baffled. "If you didn't have sex with Maggie, what's the problem?"

"I did have sex with Heather Bancroft." Mark was sheepish as he shifted on his chair. "I don't really want to admit this, for the record, but I don't see where I have a choice. Heather and Maggie were roommates. If Maggie had a plan, odds are Heather was probably in on the plan."

"Definitely."

This time when Mel and Jared exchanged looks they were less sure of what they were about to uncover.

"You'd better tell us about it," Mel said. "We can't figure this out if you hold anything back."

"I'm going to tell you," Mark promised. "I just ... can we keep it from my wife? I don't want to lose my marriage over this. I was an idiot thinking a young girl who looked like that really wanted me, but I don't want to lose my marriage for being stupid."

"I don't know that we can promise that, but we'll do our absolute best," Mel said. "I don't see why your wife would need to find out, but I can't see all the answers right now. We need a picture and you seem to be the only one who can paint it for us."

"Then I guess I'd better start painting." Mark heaved out a long-suffering sigh. "It all started when Heather and I were working late about a month ago. I thought she was being flirty but ... I'm starting to think it was something else."

Jared leaned back in his chair to listen to the tale. The story kept getting more and more convoluted and yet they had no idea which player was masquerading as a killer. They needed answers, and they needed them fast. Jared was sure that something else would happen if they didn't find out the truth sooner rather than later.

## ❧ 19 ❧

# NINETEEN

**H**arper was in the mood to fight when she landed at the barn, but Zander was too cagey to be manipulated into a screaming match when he sensed he wasn't in a position to win.

"I'll handle the perimeter." Zander was pragmatic when he wanted to be. "That way you'll be able to prod Ezra Standish across the line without risking someone coming inside and interrupting you."

Harper narrowed her eyes. "I know what you're doing."

"I'm being a good friend."

"I know what you're really doing." Harper extended a warning finger. "We're going to talk about this later."

"Talk about what?" Zander feigned innocence. "I have no idea what you're going on about."

Harper was at her limit. "I don't want you pressuring Jared. He's not ready for marriage. If you push him ... ." Harper trailed off, uncertain.

For the first time since the conversation started, Zander realized there were a bevy of emotions fueling her besides simple agitation with his busybody nature. "What do you think is going to happen?" Zander was serious. "Do you think that Jared is suddenly going to cut ties with you simply because I mess with him?"

"Of course not."

Harper's answer was a little too hurried for Zander's liking.

"No, you do." Zander made a clucking sound with his tongue. "You think I could chase away Jared."

"I do not." Harper's temper fired. "I know Jared isn't that way."

"But?"

"But ... ." Harper didn't have an answer and that frustrated her more than anything. "Just stop giving him grief. He doesn't deserve it. We're both excited about moving in together. I don't want anything to ruin our plans."

Zander's expression was hard to read as he took a long moment to look over the woman who had been his best friend for so long he couldn't remember a time in his life where she didn't claim a prominent role. "I'm not going to ruin this for you." He was serious. "That's the last thing I want. I mean ... absolute last thing. I know you love him. More importantly, I know he loves you. He's not going to run."

"I don't believe he's going to run." Harper meant it. "I don't want you forcing him into proposing before he's ready either. He would do it simply because he thought it would make me happy, and that's not what I want."

Zander widened his eyes. "What do you want?"

"I want it to happen when it's supposed to happen. Jared will know when that is. There's no reason to hurry it. We're happy. We're having a good time. We don't need to rush it."

"I never said you did."

"No, but you're trying to manipulate Jared into proposing long before he's ready and I don't like that in the least." Harper was firm. "Leave him be. I love him the way he is and want him to do things on his own timetable.

"I love you, too, but you have a tendency to push to get your own way," she continued. "That is not what I want. You need to step back and give him some breathing room. I'm not kidding."

Zander considered pushing the matter further but ultimately changed his mind. Harper's distress at the idea of forcing a timetable that Jared wasn't ready for was interesting – something he would have to give a lot of thought to later – but she was obviously serious and the last thing he wanted was to rain on her parade. "I won't push him."

"Thank you." Harper moved to climb out of his truck. "Now, let's get our stuff and get this over with. We have another tour tonight and then that's it. The rest of the Halloween season will belong to us ... including the big town costume party, which I'm really looking forward to attending with Jared this year."

"Then let's get this done." Zander was all business. "I'll run the perimeter and leave you to handle the ghost. If you need me go ahead and call."

"I'm sure I can handle this one alone."

"I'm sure you can, too. Still ... I'm supposed to be your backup. That's my job."

Harper took them both by surprise when she rolled to the balls of her feet and planted a kiss on Zander's cheek. "You're good at your job ... at least most of the time."

"All of the time," Zander corrected. "I'm a freaking maestro when it comes to being your backup."

"I couldn't agree more." Harper said the words, but they were lacking in fortitude. "Let's get this show on the road, shall we?"

"Sure." Zander bobbed his head agreeably. "After that, we're going to talk about what great backup I am even though you don't seem to believe it."

Harper rolled her eyes. "I should've seen that coming."

"You definitely should have."


**HEATHER WAS A BASKET OF** nerves when Mel and Jared drew her away from her window and into a small meeting room off the bank's main lobby. The look on her face reflected abject fear and Jared was sure she would crack relatively quickly.

"I don't understand why you want to talk to me." Heather wrung her hands together as she sat across the table and studied Jared and Mel's serious faces. "I haven't done anything."

"I'm kind of curious why you assume that we believe you have done something," Mel said gently. "What would lead you to believe that?"

Heather made an exasperated face. "Well, you insisted on taking me from my window even though my shift isn't done yet. That's a dead giveaway."

"Kind of," Mel agreed. "Of course, we are investigating the death of your roommate and we might simply have some follow-up questions for you. Did you consider that?"

Heather shook her head so hard the flaxen tresses flew from one side to the other. "No. You think I've done something. I haven't, though."

"Why don't you let us be the judge of that?" Jared suggested, shifting on the chair so he could get more comfortable. "We need to know when Maggie enlisted you to join her cause to rob the bank."

Before pulling Heather away from her post, Mel and Jared agreed the best way to question her was to pretend they already knew the answers. That was the tack Jared took now.

Heather's face turned sheet white. "What?"

"You heard me." Jared was calm. "We need to know when Maggie enlisted you to help with her plan and how far you guys actually plotted. We also want to know whether or not you fought because we're trying to ascertain if you had anything to do with Maggie's death."

Heather was dumbfounded. "You think I killed Maggie?"

"I think that someone killed Maggie," Jared replied evenly. "I think that you and Maggie were plotting something and that you already started implementing the plan so there was a chance you decided to cut Maggie out of the final payout simply because you were doing the work."

"I ... what?" Heather worked her jaw. "I don't even know what you're talking about."

"Mark," Mel supplied. "You seduced Mark because you wanted access to the vault key. You didn't know the vault needed two keys or you wouldn't have gone that route. You latched onto Maggie's plan to steal a key from Mark, though. Don't bother denying it."

Heather swallowed hard. "I think I need a lawyer."

"Maybe," Jared conceded. "Of course, you guys didn't really rob the bank and, according to Mark, you didn't steal his key. So far all you've done is talk big and chat about a plan that could never have worked."

Heather knit her eyebrows, frustration evident. "I told Maggie this was a stupid idea from the beginning. She refused to listen to me, though. Even worse than that she went off and got herself killed and left me behind to clean up the mess. That is so ... Maggie."

Jared managed to keep his face calm even as he internally crowed at Heather's capitulation. "Why don't you start from the beginning."

"Fine. I'm not sorry Maggie is dead, though. I can't be. She caused all this trouble and left it for me to clean up. I'm mad at her."

"I can see that."

"That doesn't mean I killed her, though," Heather added. "That's not who I am."

"Tell us the story and we'll decide where to go after that," Mel instructed. "We need to know everything, though. Don't leave out anything."

"Fine. I'll start from the beginning."

**HARPER FOUND EZRA SOON** after entering the barn. She was happy to discover that someone – although she had no idea who – had been through the space with garbage bags and cleaning supplies since her visit earlier in the week.

"This looks better, huh?" Harper offered up a bright smile for Ezra as she dug in her satchel for a dreamcatcher and studied the taciturn ghost. "At least the kids came back and cleaned up. That has to make you happy."

Ezra shrugged, noncommittal. He looked solid enough except for the times he drifted in front of the window and the bright sunshine caused him to all but evaporate. "I still don't think they should be out here doing what they're doing," he complained. "Back in my day, that sort of thing never happened."

"What never happened?" Harper was legitimately curious as she scuffed her foot against the dirt floor and knelt to take a look at the ground. "I don't think I'm following you."

"The fornication and debauchery," Ezra hissed, his voice low. "That stuff didn't go on when I was a youngster."

Harper snorted. This was hardly the first time she'd heard something similar from a ghost who grew up in another generation. "Do you want to know something? I don't believe that. I think you had just as much debauchery in your time as we do now. It just so happens that it occurred in different ways and there was no social media so it was easier to keep secret."

"What makes you say that?"

"I've heard the stories." Harper straightened her shoulders. "Do you know who came in and cleaned up? I didn't even hear who this year's party organizers were. I guess that means I'm getting old."

"I didn't take time to learn their names," Ezra replied, irritation bubbling up. "Why would I? They all look and sound the same to me. None of them have jobs. None of them have kids to care for even though they're of proper breeding age. It's unseemly."

Harper didn't want to laugh – if only because she knew it would further irritate Ezra – but she couldn't stop herself. "I think you're taking life way too seriously. Things are different now. Women don't get married as soon as they graduate high school. They're not simply looking for a husband to take care of them."

"And what is wrong with marrying right out of high school? That's when I got married."

"I'm not saying there's anything wrong with it," Harper clarified. "I'm saying things have changed. Women can be whatever they want in this brave new world ... and that includes wives and mothers or businesswomen. Me, for example, I chose to use my gift to help ghosts. Back in the day, I'm sure a woman would've been locked up if she said she could see and talk to ghosts."

"And rightly so," Ezra muttered, eliciting a smile from Harper.

"I'm just saying that things aren't the same as when you were alive," Harper noted. "I would like to point out that you're a ghost and I'm talking to you, so that proves I really do have a gift. That's neither here nor there, though.

"As for times changing, you guys had parties and debauchery back in the day," she continued. "You guys were much better about hiding it and keeping secrets, though. This is the information generation and everything they do or say gets put on Facebook. I don't necessarily think it's bad – although I'm not always for it – but it's not something to get worked up about."

"If you say so." Ezra rolled his eyes as he drifted to the window and looked out at the empty property where his house used to stand. "You said you were going to come back and help me cross over. Is that what you're doing now?"

"Pretty much." Harper bobbed her head. "I didn't want to forget you and I know you've been here a long time. I can help you go some-place better ... I mean, if you want to."

"And this better place, where is it? You're talking about Heaven, right?"

Harper wasn't sure how to answer. She was never comfortable discussing religion with charges. Heck, she wasn't comfortable discussing religion with random people. She was a big fan of letting people believe what they wanted to believe. That didn't mean avoiding Ezra's question was wise or warranted.

"I don't know," she answered after a beat. "I've obviously never been there so I can't say with any degree of certainty that it's Heaven. I think that it probably is, though. I think it's definitely a better place no matter what you call it."

"How can you possibly know that?" Ezra looked genuinely interested.

"Because in the brief moments when I see it, all I feel is peace." Harper opted for honesty. "It seems like a great place."

"I don't know." Ezra mimed scrubbing his hand over the back of his head, a gesture Harper was certain he picked up in life and carried over to death. She found the idea that habits stuck with souls to be quaint and alluring. "What if I don't like it over there?"

Harper held her palms out and shrugged. "I don't know. Do you like it here?"

"I ... this is my home."

"Is it?" Harper challenged. "I've always thought of a home as a place where the people you love reside. Home isn't a building ... or a house. It's not four walls and a roof. Home is where your heart is most comfortable.

"For you, I think that was the house you shared with your wife," she continued. "I know that house is long since gone – and I'm going to guess your wife is, too – but that doesn't mean you can't go home again."

Ezra adopted a thoughtful expression. "Do you really think my wife is on this other side you keep talking about?"

Harper nodded. "I think that's a good bet. If you don't want to cross over, though, I won't make you." She was sincere. "You're not hurting anyone. You're not terrorizing the populace. If you want to stay here, that's your choice. I won't force you to make a decision."

"Well, that's nice I guess," Ezra grumbled, causing Harper to have to swallow a smile. "I need a moment to think, though. Can you give me a moment?"

"Absolutely." Harper nodded and moved to the window, grinning when she saw Zander pacing in the high grass, his phone stuck to his ear. "I wonder who he's talking to."

"Who?" Ezra followed her gaze. "Isn't that your friend who likes boys? Why do you care who he's talking to? I thought you were with the other guy."

"I am with the other guy." Harper dragged her eyes from the window and focused on Ezra. She half expected the ghost to say something derisive about Zander's sexual orientation, but he merely looked thoughtful instead. "Ironically, though, my idea of Heaven would involve being with both of them on the other side even though Zander and I don't roll that way."

"I can see that." Ezra's tone wasn't dismissive or judgmental. "You love him ... just in a different way."

"That's exactly how I feel." Harper desperately wanted Ezra to move on – mostly because she felt sorry for him being alone – but she didn't want to push him before he was ready. "What do you think your wife has been doing all this time without you? Do you think she's waiting on the other side? Do you think she's been patient or agitated?"

Ezra held his palms out and shrugged. "I honestly don't know how she's been. If I had to guess, though, she's probably been cursing my name while waiting for me. She was never known for her patience."

"So maybe you shouldn't keep her waiting any longer."

"Maybe." Ezra clearly wasn't ready to make up his mind. "Tell me more about you. I listened that day you were out here with those two guys. My understanding is that you live with one of them but are moving in with the other. How come you just don't marry the one guy?"

Now it was Harper's turn to make a face. "Has Zander been out here telling you what to say to me? If he wasn't afraid of dirt and bugs, I would almost think he had all of this planned."

"I have no idea what you're talking about. In fact ... ." Ezra broke off, his gaze landing on a spot over Harper's left shoulder.

Harper jerked her head in that direction, convinced she would find Zander waiting there as he tried to hurry her along. Instead, she met Maggie Harris's steady gaze and frowned. "What are you doing here, Maggie?"

"I was looking for you."

"Me?" Harper was legitimately surprised. "Why were you looking for me?"

"I remember what happened."

"You do?" Harper's heart rate ticked up a notch. "You remember who killed you? Who was it?"

"I was in the cemetery a bit ago." Maggie seemed lost in thought. "He was there. He's been there a lot over the past few days. I didn't remember he was the one, though, until ... well, today."

Harper nodded encouragingly. "Okay. Who is it?"

"I don't know his name."

Harper's lips curved down. "You don't know the name of the man who killed you?"

Maggie shook her head. "He's here, though. He followed me."

Harper was ridiculously confused. "The man who killed you followed your ghostly form from the cemetery to here? I don't under-stand. That doesn't make any sense."

"He's like you."

"Like me?" Harper licked her lips, unsure. "Do you mean he can see ghosts?"

Maggie nodded. "That's exactly what I mean. He's here. He came for me, followed me. He's looking for you now, though."

Even though her mind refused to grasp what Maggie was saying, Harper recognized fear when she saw it and she hurried back to the window so she could look out. Instead of seeing Zander's reassuring figure, though, the area in front of the barn was completely empty ... except for a car Harper didn't recognize.

Her heart skipped a beat as multiple information sources collided.

"Who is it? Who followed you, Maggie?"

"I don't know but he's here ... and he's coming." Maggie started to disappear. "I knew I was better off not remembering, by the way. I wish I would've followed my instincts."

And just like that, Maggie was gone and the barn door was swinging open.

Harper swallowed hard. "Oh, this can't be good."

## 20

### TWENTY

Harper instinctively headed toward the door, her hand digging into her pocket for her phone. She was annoyed at Maggie's disappearance, until the ghost suddenly reappeared with no warning and she walked directly through her, causing a chill. "What the ... ?"

"You should run."

Harper didn't doubt that, but she couldn't run until she knew exactly what she was dealing with. She focused on the door opening as she clumsily fumbled in her pocket for her phone.

"Who is here?"

It was a stupid question, but Harper felt a desperate need to fill the conversational gap. Maggie didn't have a chance to answer – or brush off the question – because a figure appeared in the doorway. It was a familiar face, and it threw Harper for a loop.

"Gary?"

Of all the people she expected to find, Gary Conner was the last one on a rather short list. In fact, Harper was so dumbfounded she could do nothing but openly gape.

"Ms. Harlow." Gary glanced around the barn, his eyes darting in a myriad of different directions. "I guess I should've realized you were in here when I ran into your friend outside."

*Zander!* Harper's heart gave a lurch. She didn't understand what was going on but recognized she was in a vulnerable position. "Is he still out there?" Harper did her best to appear calm. "I'm surprised he didn't call out to me when you pulled up. Did you talk to him?"

"He's ... otherwise engaged." Gary's demeanor was hard for Harper to read, but when his gaze landed on the spot to her left – the spot where Maggie's ghost floated – Harper had the distinct impression that things were about to shift ... and not necessarily in a good way. "You don't have to worry about him. He's out of the picture, so to speak."

Gary's chilling tone was enough to make Harper's blood run cold. "Did you do something to him?"

"Oh, all manner of things." Gary's lips curved. "What are you even doing here? I must confess, this is not how I planned on spending my day."

"It's not how I planned on spending my day either." Harper moved to her left when Gary took a tentative step forward, making sure to keep a reasonable distance between them. "I guess we're both off our games, huh?"

"I never really considered this a game." Gary kept his eyes on Harper's face, his mouth moving occasionally, as if keeping up some internal debate only he could hear. "In fact, I came to you in the first place because I was having a crisis of faith. You kind of blew me off – that's your way, though, isn't it? – and now we're here. I find the entire thing ... interesting."

Harper didn't know what to make of the statement. "You killed Maggie, didn't you?"

"I protected myself," Gary corrected. "There's a difference."

"How so?"

"I didn't go to that cemetery looking for her," Gary answered, shifting a tad closer and forcing Harper to take a step in retreat. He seemed to be enjoying his power over her, something Harper wasn't keen to spend too much time reflecting upon. "I didn't expect to kill her that night, in case you're wondering. I was as surprised as her when we crossed paths."

Harper licked her lips as she debated how to proceed. The Gary Conner she knew from cemetery tours was not a killer. He was an annoying man who always seemed eager to engage in debates about the paranormal, always questioning the very existence of ghosts, but he was not a murderer. How he turned into the predator Harper could clearly see now was beyond her limits of understanding.

"So, she went to the cemetery after all," Harper mused, buying time. "Did she drive herself there?"

"You'll have to ask her."

"Okay." Harper flicked her eyes to Maggie. "Did you drive to the cemetery?" Harper wasn't putting on a show as much as testing Gary. She had a theory and she needed help from the two ghosts in the building to prove it.

Maggie nodded. "I drove there. I was supposed to meet someone."

"Danny Wood?"

Maggie widened her eyes. "How did you know I was seeing him?"

"Because Jared and Mel have been doing endless legwork," Harper replied, shaking her head. "They know about your plotting with Jay Forrester and Danny Wood. They know that you were going to attempt to steal from the bank. They even know how some of those plans were – or were not, in this particular case – were shaking out."

"I guess that's supposed to make me feel bad, huh?" Maggie pursed her lips. "I don't. That money in the bank was insured. No one was going to get hurt if I took it. Insurance companies are full of fat morons who do nothing but sit back and make money hand over fist. My plan was harmless."

Harper opened her mouth to respond, but Gary beat her to it.

"Harmless, huh?" Gary made an odd sound in the back of his throat, as if he were trying to dislodge something stuck there. "People would've lost their jobs over that if you managed to carry it out. How is that harmless?"

Harper almost felt triumphant when Gary answered. Then she remembered her predicament. "You heard her."

"What?" Gary's face was blank.

"You heard her," Harper repeated. "You can hear Maggie. She said you followed her here. Does that mean you can see her, too?"

"Oh, *that*." Gary's face reflected mild boredom and disinterest. "Yeah. I can see her, too. Is that important to you? I can see and hear her. It's ... ridiculous."

"Why is it ridiculous?" Harper knew she needed to buy time. Jared was aware of her location, but he had no reason to believe she was in trouble. She had a phone in her pocket, but if she pulled it out with the intention to call her boyfriend, Gary was liable to react in a violent way. That meant she needed to put space between herself and Gary before making the attempt. To do that, she needed to lull him into a false sense of security. The only way she knew to achieve that was through conversation.

"Because ghosts aren't real," Gary replied simply. "They're not real and I know it."

Harper furrowed her brow. "You heard Maggie speak, though. You followed her from the cemetery to here. She's real. I can see her, too."

The look Gary graced Harper with was almost piteous. "Well, maybe you have a brain tumor like I do. I would suggest going to the doctor to have yourself checked out but you're not going to be around long enough to do it and I don't want to give you false hope."

Harper swallowed hard. That was a lot of information to digest in one rambling statement. "Tumor? You have a brain tumor?"

Gary bobbed his head. "Inoperable. In six months, I won't even be able to stand on my own. Three months after that I'll be bedridden. Three months after that I'll be worm food."

"Thanks for that bright and shiny outlook on life," Harper muttered, shaking her head. "How do you know you have a brain tumor?"

"Because I went to the doctor when I started seeing ghosts," Gary replied matter-of-factly. "They were everywhere. I couldn't even walk out my door without seeing them. I knew something was wrong.

"At first, my doctor thought I was having some sort of mental breakdown," he continued. "He suggested lithium ... and maybe even a stint in a locked ward for a bit so I could talk about what I was seeing with a licensed professional. I was so adamant, though, he eventually delved deeper. That's when he found the tumor."

Harper was legitimately confused. "But Maggie is really here." She gestured toward the quiet ghost, who gazed on her killer with furious eyes but otherwise remained silent. "I can see her, too, and I don't have a tumor."

"So you think."

"I'm pretty sure that's true," Harper countered. "I've been able to see ghosts since I was a little kid. I've been in the hospital a few times since then, too. I doubt very much I've been living with a tumor for the bulk of my life without anyone noticing."

Gary tilted his head to the side, considering. "I guess that's a fair point. I see ghosts because of my tumor, though. I know it."

"But ... if we're seeing the same ghost, how is that possible? Maybe you have a tumor *and* you can see ghosts. Perhaps those two things aren't related. Have you ever considered that?"

Gary immediately started shaking his head. "No. Ghosts aren't real."

Harper felt as if she was mired in quicksand and sinking rapidly. "I'm really lost here, Gary, so I need you to start from the beginning. I want to help you and I'm not sure I can do that if I don't understand what you're thinking and feeling."

"It's fairly simple. What I'm thinking is that I'm going to have to kill you or spend the rest of my life – however short – in prison. No one wants that. What I'm feeling is that your voice is like nails on a chalkboard and I want you to shut up."

"That's not very helpful."

"I didn't know I was supposed to be helpful. When did we agree upon that?"

Harper bit back a sigh and tried to ignore how sweaty her palms were. She had a chance to get out of this. She merely had to wait for an opening. "I need to know why you killed Maggie," she said, changing tactics. "I didn't suspect you. Not even a little. I need to know why you would possibly want to kill a girl you didn't even know."

"What makes you think I didn't know her?"

"She told me you didn't."

"Ah, well she's right. I didn't know her." Gary's hands were devoid of a weapon but that didn't mean he wasn't armed. Harper watched him closely – paying particular attention to the waistband of his khakis as he shifted his hips back and forth – and prayed he was unarmed so she would have an easier chance of overpowering him. "I wasn't looking for her in the cemetery that night. In fact, I thought she was someone else entirely."

The words were like a punch in the gut to Harper as Gary's eyes suggestively snagged with hers. "You thought she was someone else?" Harper cast Maggie a sidelong look. The girl was young, in her twenties, and tall. She had shoulder-length blond hair and slim hips. Realization hit Harper like a brick to the head. "You thought she was me."

"And, finally, you're starting to catch on," Gary intoned, his eyes gleaming. "I was indeed there looking for you. That was the day my doctor gave me my prognosis. I knew I was sick before, you see, but I kept telling myself I would somehow be able to survive what was to come.

"I knew odds weren't in my favor, but I really believed things would get better once I knew what was wrong with me," he continued. "I thought I would have to undergo an operation and a long recovery, but after that the ghosts would be gone. Unfortunately, my tumor is too big. There is no operation that can save me."

"And I'm legitimately sorry about that," Harper offered. "It doesn't seem fair that you should suffer this way and then be told there's no way out. That still doesn't explain why you killed Maggie. That doesn't explain why you're here threatening me now."

"I killed Maggie because I thought she was you. I already told you that. I went to the cemetery to talk to my parents – they've been gone a number of years now – and I was really upset. I wanted someone to make things better, even if they weren't really there. I needed to talk things out. Then I saw you."

Harper frowned. "You thought you saw me."

"You were walking through the cemetery and all I saw was red," Gary explained. "I saw red and went to chase you down, only it wasn't you. I realized too late it was someone else, but I was so angry I couldn't stop myself from taking out my frustration anyway."

Harper felt sick to her stomach. "You strangled her."

"She almost looked like you while I did it. That made me feel better."

"And that's why you were on the tour the following night," Harper supplied. "You wanted to be the one to discover her body. You wiped her down with cleaning supplies, those germ wipes you get at the grocery store, but you needed to be sure no one would question you should some of your DNA be discovered. That's why you went off in the direction you did even though it didn't make sense."

"Pretty much." Gary wasn't bothered by Harper's tone. "I knew once I killed her that I had to cover my tracks. A brain tumor isn't going to keep me out of prison and I have a lot of living I want to do in the next six months."

"What about the living I wanted to do?" Maggie asked, her voice raspy. "I had a lot of living I wanted to do, too."

"From what I can tell, you were a drain on society," Gary replied, blasé. "You would've ended up trying to trap a man with a pregnancy to steal his money and then probably gone on welfare or something. I don't think the world is weeping over your demise."

Harper was insulted on Maggie's behalf. "She was young. You don't know what she would've grown to be. All you know is that you were angry with me and I don't even understand why you were feeling that way."

"You don't understand?" Gary let loose with a low snarl. "You don't understand why I was upset? How many of your stupid tours have I been on over the years?"

Harper frantically did the math in her head. "I don't know. Like five, at least I think."

"Try seventeen." Gary was a man running out of patience, something his tapping foot clearly signified. "I went on my first tour four weeks after I saw my first ghost. I was looking for answers and saw your ad in the newspaper. I thought it was divine intervention."

"You never mentioned it, though," Harper pointed out. "You never told me what you saw. How did you expect me to help you if I didn't even know you were having a problem?"

"What did you think all those long discussions were about?" Gary challenged. "Did you honestly think I wanted to discuss the nature of the universe with you? I needed to know what was true. Whenever I asked you a question – like how did you manage to get your power in the first place – you completely ignored me. No, that's being kind. It was more that you rolled your eyes and verbally swatted me away."

Harper wanted to argue with the assertion, but she wasn't sure she could. She remembered being frustrated with Gary to the point where she and Zander made fun of him behind his back. She remembered rolling her eyes so many times when the man opened his mouth that she'd honestly turned it into a game of sorts. The realization didn't make her proud.

"Yeah. You're remembering." Gary was smug as he folded his arms over his chest. "I wasn't at those tours because I had a crush on you like poor Colin, or because I was really interested in why that Randy Johnson douche spent all his time throwing grave decorations at people. I wanted answers on the bigger picture."

Harper felt beyond helpless. "And what made you think I would have those answers?"

"You're the expert, aren't you? You're the ghost hunter to end all ghost hunters. You're such a real deal they've written about you in the newspaper. If you didn't have answers for me, who was I supposed to turn to?"

"I ... ." Harper didn't have an answer. "I don't know. You were in a bad position. That doesn't mean what you did to Maggie is right. It's not forgivable."

"And what about what was done to me?" Gary challenged, his face twisting with anger as spittle formed at the corners of his mouth. "How is it fair that I saw ghosts and it caused me to have a brain tumor? Why did it happen to me?"

"I think you're tying one of those things to the other without proof," Harper shot back. "Maybe you could always see ghosts and never realized it until recently. I always thought I saw my first ghost at five but, come to find out, that wasn't true. I didn't realize that until recently when I ran into a ghost I met long before I remembered seeing what I thought was my first ghost.

"The same could be true of you," she continued. "You might've

177

been able to see ghosts your whole life but only realized it when you got sick because the veil between the two worlds was somehow thinner. That doesn't mean that you're dying because you can see ghosts."

"And it doesn't mean I'm not." Gary pressed his lips together as he regarded Harper. "I didn't come here for you today. I want you to know that. I came here for her." He pointed toward Maggie's furious image. "I wanted to talk to her about what happened. It's not that I needed to apologize or anything, mind you, but I figured I owed her some sort of explanation. She ran from me, though, and I find it interesting that she ran straight to you."

"And why do you find that interesting?"

"Because you were the one I was looking for that night," Gary replied honestly. "I was angry at you and I took it out on someone else. It made me feel better. Can you imagine, knowing that, how much better I'm going to feel after exerting my anger on a real target this time? It's as if fate intervened."

Harper was taken aback and took another step away from the crazed man, inadvertently running into the bar. "This isn't fate. This is your madness."

"I think I'm fine with that." Gary reached into his pocket. Harper wasn't sure what he was trying to grab, but she realized she was officially out of time. "Now, if you could stand still, this will be a lot easier."

"I don't think so." Harper moved to scramble away from the bar, but she didn't get a chance because another figure appeared in the open doorway. This one was taller, his footing uneven, and he looked absolutely furious. "Zander?"

Gary sensed they were no longer alone and moved to swivel, but it was already too late. Zander smashed the branch he carried – something he must have picked up outside – against the back of Gary's head and caused him to pitch forward. He lashed out again as Gary staggered, just to make sure.

Zander swiped at the blood along the side of his face, grimacing at the grime and filth on his fingers, and then sneered at Harper. "You're welcome."

Harper exhaled a shaky breath. "I ... thank you. Are you okay?"

"I need a doctor."

"I'll call right now." Harper's fingers shook as she tried to look anywhere but at Gary's crumpled body. "He's not dead, is he?"

"No, but he deserves to be. He hit me from behind. He deserves a lot more than I gave him."

"I'll call for help."

"Good." Zander slowly sank to the floor, ignoring the dirt and focusing his full attention on Gary. "Now that I'm your hero, I think we should talk about the color pink while waiting for the cavalry."

Harper knew he was talking simply to have something to focus on so she decided to give him what he needed ... an argument. "Don't push me."

"Oh, I think I've earned a fantastic shade of pink."

"It's not going to happen."

"Just you wait."

# TWENTY-ONE

"How do I look?"

Zander stepped out of his bedroom shortly after five the next day and offered Harper, Shawn, and Jared an expectant look. His head injury – which the doctor said he was lucky to have survived with no ill effects – forced a change in costume. The cowboy hat he wore, full of pink and purple sparkles, made Harper smile.

"You look like a rhinestone cowboy."

"That's exactly what I was going for." Zander let out a groan as he settled on the couch next to Shawn and rested his feet on the coffee table. "When are we leaving for the town party?"

"It doesn't start for another hour," Harper reminded him. She was halfway prepared – her fairy makeup highlighting her angular features – but she'd yet to slip into the pretty costume and instead preferred lounging around in her robe. "We'll be on time. Don't worry."

"Do I look worried?"

He looked tired, Harper internally noted. She'd been a nervous wreck when calling for help the previous day and refused to leave Zander's side until the doctor assured her he wasn't going to lose consciousness and never wake up. That was long after Jared and Shawn showed up to offer emotional support, both of them realizing quickly that Harper needed to focus on Zander so Gary's motivations for murder wouldn't cause her to melt down.

"We were talking about Gary," Shawn volunteered, ignoring the dark look Harper shot him as he stroked his hand over Zander's forearm. "It seems he's claiming to be innocent despite admitting everything to Harper. Jared was just telling us about this morning's interrogation."

"I thought Gary was in the hospital," Zander said, distaste evident. "He was claiming memory loss from when I hit him last time I checked."

"He's still claiming that," Jared supplied. "He says he has no idea why he was at the barn and has no recollection of attacking Harper."

"He didn't technically attack me," Harper pointed out. "He was gearing up to do it when Zander swooped in and saved me." She offered her best friend a frothy smile. "My hero."

"Ugh." Jared made a face. "How long are you going to keep placating him by calling him that?"

"Until he stops demanding a pink kitchen in return for his heroics," Harper replied.

"Oh, I'll never give up on that." Zander managed a flirty wink. "I've yet to begin to fight on that front."

"I can't tell you how much dread that fills me with," Jared supplied, running his fingers over Harper's hand as he leaned back in his seat. "As for Gary, I'm not sure how much his sudden memory loss is going to matter. The doctor checked him over and he wasn't lying about having an inoperable brain tumor."

Harper wasn't sure how she was supposed to feel about that. "Is it wrong that part of me feels sorry for him?"

"No. I think we all feel sorry for him. He still murdered an innocent woman." Jared lifted her hand and pressed a kiss to the palm. "You have a big heart. That's one of the first things I noticed about you ... besides how smoking hot you are. I think it's normal to feel sympathy for someone in Gary's position."

Harper snorted as Zander rolled his eyes.

"Maggie is still dead," Jared pointed out. "She'll never have a chance to be more than what she turned out to be. I think that's as sad as what's happening to Gary."

"Speaking of Maggie, you never really got into a lot of detail about what happened with Heather," Shawn pointed out. "What did she have to say about her actions?"

"She said that she was reticent about sleeping with Mark, but she agreed to do it because she didn't want to be left out in case Maggie and Danny actually managed to pull off their plan," Jared replied. "It wasn't that she wanted to rob the bank as much as she didn't want to be the person who didn't get rich from robbing the bank."

"That's pretty sad, too," Harper said.

"It is," Jared agreed. "She's been fired, by the way. She threatened Mark with telling his wife about the affair if he didn't back down, but he had no choice. He has a fiduciary responsibility to the bank clients so Heather had to go."

"Do you think Heather will tell his wife?" Shawn asked. "I mean ... I don't know her. Is she that sort of person?"

"A week ago, I would've said no," Harper answered. "Everything I've learned about both Heather and Maggie this week makes me think otherwise. I think it's entirely possible Heather will tell Mark's wife about the affair. Of course, since Mark is a big cheater, I don't have a lot of sympathy for him."

"I hate it when things work out this way," Zander lamented as he stared at the ceiling. "I much prefer it when the ghosts we're supposed to help are innocent and we can be sure we're doing good."

"Ezra was innocent," Harper pointed out. "In fact, after witnessing what happened in the barn yesterday, he said that made his decision to cross over easier. He doesn't care how annoying his wife was in life – and he stressed she was really mean and bitter when she wanted to be – he thinks being with her is better than being alone."

"When are you going over there to help him cross over?" Jared asked. "I'll go with you when it's time. I don't want you going to that barn alone."

"I already helped him cross over while you were busy at the hospital this morning."

Jared wrinkled his forehead. "Why would you do that without me?"

"Because there was no danger and that's my job," Harper replied simply. "You were busy. Zander was sleeping in. Instead of bothering him and Shawn – which I would've done if I didn't leave the house – I decided to be productive. I felt better after helping Ezra. I refuse to apologize for that."

Jared pinched the bridge of his nose. "I don't want you to apologize. It's just ... I thought you might be upset about going there by yourself. I know you've been struggling with what Gary told you. You don't have to hide that from me. Anyone in your position would be upset."

"It's not that I feel upset as much as I feel guilty." Harper chose her words carefully. "I know you're going to say I didn't cause Maggie's death – and I get that – but I still feel guilty. I can't get around those feelings because they're a part of me. Maggie only died because Gary was confused and thought she looked like me."

"Maggie died because Gary is a sick man," Jared countered, forcing Harper's eyes to him by tilting her chin. "Gary is dying and wanted to take it out on someone. We'll never know if the brain tumor confused him to the point where he really thought the ghosts were a byproduct of the tumor of if he was simply looking for a reason to justify his actions.

"What happened that night in the cemetery is not your fault and I'm going to be angry if you blame yourself," he continued. "You didn't cause it to happen. Maggie was at the wrong place at the wrong time. It could be argued that it wouldn't have happened if she didn't get drunk and decide to meet Danny there to talk about their potential bank robbery.

"By the way, we talked to Danny again today and asked why he conveniently forgot to mention he was supposed to meet Maggie that night," Jared said. "He said that he forgot and didn't bother to head over there because he thought Maggie would be otherwise engaged. I'm not sure if I believe that, but I have to think he would've stepped in if he showed up and realized she was being attacked. Of course, with this group, that could simply be wishful thinking."

"Will anything happen to him?" Shawn asked.

Jared shrugged. "I don't know. We're leaving that up to the prosecutor. That whole little group had bad intentions, but they never got so far as to actually launch a plan."

"Heather did," Zander reminded him. "She had sex with Mark."

"She did, but Mark didn't share any information with her and she never got as far as drugging him and stealing his key," Jared responded. "I mean ... she didn't even get as far as researching drugs to knock him out. It's all a slippery slope. Where does intent meet action?"

"You're just glad you're not going to be a part of it going forward, aren't you?" Harper queried.

"I am glad that I can focus on you and put this ugly mess behind us," Jared agreed. "We have a party tonight – where I believe I'm going to sneak a dance or two with my pretty fairy – and then tomorrow I have people coming over to start taking the furniture out of the new house."

Harper brightened considerably at the news. "You didn't tell me that."

"I wanted it to be a surprise." Jared's grin was lazy. "After that, I thought we could have a nice lunch together – I'll treat – and then we'll start seriously considering paint colors." Jared extended a finger when Zander opened his mouth. "Pink is off the list for the kitchen. Let it go."

"You guys are absolutely no fun," Zander grumbled as he folded his arms over his chest.

"That sounds like a good plan." Harper rested the side of her head against Jared's shoulder. "I do have one more question, though. After that, if we never talk about Gary again, it will be too soon."

"Okay. Lay it on me."

"Did Gary say why he chose to dump Maggie's body so close to the Standish mausoleum? I mean ... I thought for sure that had to be symbolic or something. Now I'm starting to wonder if it was simply a coincidence."

"He didn't admit to killing Maggie so I doubt very much he'll ever explain why he picked that location," Jared replied. "I don't have an answer for you. We'll probably never know."

"He probably picked that spot because it was near the end of the tour," Zander volunteered. "He was with us enough times to know where we ended things. That was a convenient location."

"I guess." Harper shifted so she could gaze into Jared's worried eyes. "I'm okay. You don't have to worry."

"It's my job to worry. That's what happens when you love someone."

"I don't feel guilty the way you think I feel guilty," Harper clarified. "I'll always wonder what could have been, though. It's not something I'll be able to shake."

"I don't want you dwelling on it." Jared was firm. "I want you to open yourself up to fun. You told me this is your favorite night of the year. You're all sparkly and I've seen that costume in the bedroom. It has wings. You can't have a bad time when you're wearing wings."

Harper finally mustered a real smile. "I plan on having a good time. I plan on stuffing my face with chocolate and wings. I also plan on dancing with a very handsome man."

"She's talking about me," Zander interjected.

Jared ignored him. "I plan on having a good time, too. I guess it's good we're on the same wavelength. I'm more worried about tomorrow than today, though. You'll be busy tonight. I don't want you changing your mind and starting to blame yourself tomorrow. Can you promise me that won't happen?"

Harper nodded, solemn. "I promise not to blame myself. Besides, I won't have time. It's a brave new world and there are always ghosts out there who need help. I need to focus on them rather than myself."

"That sounds easier said than done, but I'm going to let it go ... for now." Jared gave her a soft kiss. "We have a house to focus on, too. That's something to look forward to."

"That's definitely something to look forward to."

"I think you should look forward to the pink kitchen," Zander pressed. "That will make everyone feel better."

"Don't make me rope and hogtie you," Jared warned. "I'm this close to doing it."

"Promises, promises."

The group dissolved into laughter, happy in the moment to simply be together. Trouble would come again, but for now, they were safe and happy. They couldn't ask for more than that.

98555282R00114

Made in the USA
Columbia, SC
27 June 2018